ALICE'S EROTIC ADVENTURES THROUGH THE MIRROR

Alice's Erotic Adventures

Book 2

LIZ ADAMS

ALICE'S EROTIC ADVENTURES THROUGH THE MIRROR
(ALICE'S EROTIC ADVENTURES, BOOK 2)

Published by: Barany Publishing
ISBN-13: 978-1-944841-01-0

ALICE'S EROTIC ADVENTURES THROUGH THE MIRROR

Alice's Erotic Adventures

Book 2

CONTENTS

The Poem Opens

You wake up in the morn each day,
Half past the daily time,
You dress yourself in daily clothes
And wear your daily grime.
You hope your face, he will adore.
Each day your soul, he does ignore.

The birds they chant their humdrum songs
As though they follow orders.
The sun it rains its dripping rays
Upon your heavy shoulders.
There is no joy. There is no laughter.
You cannot find the path you're after.

And when the birds have closed their songs,
The sun, it's passed away,
And when your man comes home to you
Just like he does each day,
You feed on tasteless pleasantries,
And eat your tasteless memories.

The time has come to go to bed
You strip and take your station.
You let him touch you in the hopes
He'll show appreciation.
He fills your holes until your sore
As if it were a proper chore.

The one solution to resolve
Such days of love ignored,
To have a life of admiration,
One so much adored,
Is just to ask yourself one query,
Answer truthfully and clearly.

To go from days of loneliness
To those of joy and laughter,
The simplest question you can ask,
The hardest one to answer:
"Who am I and what can I do
To make myself be known to you?"

1. Troublemakers

Put your hand over your heart.
Does it beat in love?
Or does it beat in fear?

AFTER her family had gone to bed, Alice Dellid snuck out of her bedroom, just as she had every night since she returned home from university for winter break. She stole downstairs with careful steps. From the foot of the stairs, the front door was just a short distance away.

"Ahem." It was Barbara, the maid.

Alice stopped dead.

Barbara was folding clean tablecloths near the front hallway and didn't glance at Alice. Did Barbara even know Alice was there? Perhaps the old lady really was just clearing her throat.

Alice remained still. She was as close to Barbara as she was to the front door. Any sudden movements might get Barbara's attention. If Barbara were to spot her, she was the type of woman who would let everyone in the house know about it, starting with Alice's father.

Alice eyed her wool coat. It hung by the front door by her boots. She would need it to protect herself from the blistering cold. The goal seemed so simple: get the jacket, grab the boots, go outside.

Alice eased closer to the front door, placing one step in front of her. Then another.

Squeak!

Damn floorboards. Alice froze, now in clear view of Barbara if the maid raised her head. Thankfully, she didn't. Barbara was hard of hearing.

The front door was two arm's lengths away, but all Barbara had to do was turn her head to spot Alice. Biting her lip, Alice pulled together her options and thought through a quick vote. The back door won as the better candidate.

Alice raised her foot off the floorboard. It squeaked again. Alice didn't move. Barbara continued folding the linen.

Pivoting on one foot, Alice faced the hallway that lead to the back door. She padded barefoot in that direction. Gently. Quietly. Then she was out of

Barbara's view and minced to the back of the house. Thank goodness Barbara's hearing had diminished over the years.

JACK hurried down the lamp-lit street. He had to finish quickly to be back in time for Alice. He turned off the busy street into the alley, hoisting his burlap sack over his shoulder.

Everybody knew you should stay away from Vagabond Alley. Too many drunks, beggars, and runaways spent their nights there when they finished their daily job of asking for spare change.

"Jack!" Harry peeked out of his cardboard home wearing a sparse-toothed grin.

"How ya doin', Harry?" Jack reached into his sack.

"Can't complain. The clouds are out, keeping me toes and bullocks nice and warm. Like a blanket in the sky."

Jack handed him a bread roll and a chunk of cold chicken breast. "Sounds good."

"Bless yer heart, Jack." Harry took the food in his gloved hands and sunk his teeth into the white meat.

Jack eyed the far end of the alley. "How's the new kid?"

Harry paused his chewing and followed Jack's gaze.

"Not so good," Harry said through his mouthful. "He ain't street smart, and he ain't so chummy, know what I mean?"

Jack nodded. Suspicious of strangers. Offering a helping hand to the kid would be difficult.

"Doesn't talk much." Harry swallowed his food. "Not sure he'll last the winter."

"Thanks, Harry. Keep warm, okay?"

Jack made his way through the alley, greeting each habitant with a roll and a piece of chicken, the leftovers from the Dellid's meals back at the manor house. He knew each of the homeless men by name and usually came once a week. During the winter, however, Jack visited them every night to make sure they got the nourishment they needed to survive the cold.

At the far end of the alley, the new boy lay curled into a ball, clutching his knees to his chest. His shirt and trousers were dirty, but looked expensive by their cut and fancy buttons. The clothes may have been nice for a fancy outing, but not good for surviving the cold. The kid was probably a runaway, escaping some trouble.

"Hey," Jack said with cheer in his voice. "What's your name?"

The kid didn't respond. He just raised his eyes to Jack and narrowed them with suspicion.

"Want some chicken?" Jack held out a chicken leg.

The boy didn't move, but licked his lips.

"Come on. Everyone else is enjoying theirs."

The boy sat up and eyed the others in the alley, all feasting on the food Jack brought. He snatched the chicken leg out of Jack's hands and took a healthy bite of the meat and chewed in a hurry, all manners, if he ever had any, gone.

Jack pulled out a roll from the sack. "Here's some bread to go along with that."

The kid grabbed it and kept gobbling the chicken in big hungry bites.

Jack examined him. The boy would be lucky to survive the week, the way he was dressed. He needed help. Since Alice already knew about Jack's trips to the alley, surely she'd understand letting a desperate kid spend one night in his cabin.

"You know, I have a cabin. It's small, but it's warm. How about you spend the night there?"

The boy stopped mid-chew. He held up his finger, finished chewing, swallowed, then asked, "Are you some kind of sex freak?"

Jack chuckled. "No, it's nothing like that. It's just if you want a warm place to spend the night, that's all."

"I don't see you offering that nice, warm cabin to anyone else here."

Time to be upfront. "That's because those guys

know how to survive the streets. You look like it's your first winter. That can be tough."

"Save your breath, Santa Claus. I'm not going anywhere."

Jack sighed and shrugged out of his coat, the cold air chilling his torso. "Then take this. It'll help."

The boy didn't accept the coat, he just continued eating. Jack lay the coat over the kid's legs. The kid didn't kick it off.

"I'll leave you be," Jack said.

Before Jack left, the kid asked, "Why are you doing this?" He held up the chicken and bread.

"I made a promise to myself."

The kid sneered, "What was it you promised? Did you promise to feel sorry for homeless people?"

"No," Jack said. "I promised never to forget where I came from."

Jack hustled back the way he came, through the alley and along the lamp-lit street. Passing the closed shops led to a residential area, and deeper down the winding roads, the houses were larger and scattered, surrounded by ample front lawns and long driveways. Jack sprinted the next several minutes to return to his cabin in time for Alice's visit.

*****

ALICE eased the lock on the back door and tiptoed in her bare feet across the threshold. She faced the biting chill of the night through her sheer nightgown. The cold iced her chest, but bit strongest at her knees and shins since the nightgown covered her thighs and exposed the rest of her. It didn't matter. The cold made her feel alive.

Quiet. Alice needed to stay quiet.

Outside, she pulled the door with a steady tug until it clicked closed. A high-pitched cry came from above. Startled, Alice jumped. She scanned the sky for the source of the sound.

In the tree, her tabby cat clung to a high branch, its ears flat against its head.

"Dinah," Alice whispered, rubbing her arms to stay warm. "How did you manage to sneak outside?"

Dinah glared at her, as if it were Alice's fault she was up a tree on a cold winter's night and not snug in her basket by the fire.

"I wish you'd tell me how you escaped, so I could know your trick." Alice frowned and planted a bare foot on the low branch of the tree she'd climbed so many times before. "Surely your way is sneakier than going out the front or back door."

Dinah swished her tail and said nothing, keeping her secret.

Alice gripped the trunk and climbed higher. The rough tree bark under her feet proved easier to grasp than when she wore shoes.

"I bet you climbed up there and got stuck for attention, didn't you?" Alice huffed out in a whisper as she reached the height of the manor's second floor. "It's all about Her Majesty Dinah of Dellid Manor."

"Meow."

"Hush! You'll wake up Lois and Carol." Alice glanced through the window at the nearby bedroom.

In the bedroom, her sister Lois slept cuddled beside her lover Carol. If Alice's parents ever found out that their daughter Lois was a lesbian and Carol was not just Lois's friend, but was also her paramour, they'd be furious. More furious than if her parents found out about Alice's relationship with Jack, their servant. There was no place for homosexual relationships. So Alice kept Lois's secret from their parents, and Lois kept Alice's secret.

Alice pulled herself up within reach of Dinah, plucked her cat off the branch with one sweep of her arm, and pressed the frightened creature against her shoulder.

Dinah dug in to her shoulder with her sharp claws. Alice sucked in a breath against the pain.

"Alright, troublemaker. Let's get you back inside before you turn into a catsicle."

Getting down was going to be trickier than climbing up. Alice had only three limbs to work with. The fourth, one arm, was wrapped around Dinah's furry weight.

Alice eased herself onto a lower branch, but her

foot stepped on some sharp broken limb. Ow! She stepped off but missed the handhold she usually used.

Alice snatched at whatever branch she could grab. The meager substitute bent. Alice's fist slid down the downward bending branch. She leapt to get a better foothold.

She blew out a breath. Her feet found solid purchase, her fist stopped sliding down the branch, and Dinah's claws sunk deeper into her shoulder.

Alice winced, eased herself to a more balanced position, and resumed the downward climb.

Once on firm ground, she stepped to the back door and cracked it open. A rush of inviting warm air spilled out.

Alice raised Dinah to look at her eye-to-eye. "You be good now, Your Majesty. No more gallivanting in the cold."

Alice gave her a kiss. Dinah mewed in protest. Alice shoved her prim cat inside and shut the door.

In the cold, she slid the nightgown off her shoulder and checked her wounds. Dinah made a new constellation of red dots there, but nothing serious.

In the chill winter air, clad only in Jack's favorite nightgown, she headed to Jack's cabin.

*****

JACK rushed into his cabin, glad to be out of the chilly night. He returned later than usual from visiting Vagabond Alley, but thankfully, Alice hadn't arrived yet.

Jack checked the time. She'd come within five minutes. It wasn't enough time to read a few more chapters from H. Rider Haggard's *She,* but it was enough time to read a few paragraphs.

Jack peeled off his work boots, nabbed the adventure book from his shelf, and jumped onto his creaky bed to lie down. Ah, this was the life. A roof over his head, a guarantee of food every day, a warm bed, and—the spice of all spices—Alice as his beloved.

He cracked open the book to explore a different, more dangerous world.

SNOW fell at a leisurely pace, like the clouds were saying, "Yay!" and threw confetti. Alice giggled and raced across the moist grass, careful not to step on any twigs, though it was hard to see them in the moonlit night. She carried with her both the secret of her relationship with Jack, the gardener, and the excitement of being lavished with his attention, his flowers, and his cooking.

During the summer, he had given her an abundance of loving that way, and though he had yet to give her any flowers or any of his tasty dishes this winter, he was clearly busy and would get back to his generosity one of these days. She didn't want to be a chore.

Within five minutes she arrived at his cabin and pushed the door open without knocking, just as she had the last three nights. Jack lay on his bed reading *She*.

Alice rubbed the shivers off her arms and stomped her feet to get some feeling back in her toes. "Hello!"

Jack grunted his welcome, then said, "Just a second. I want to finish this paragraph."

"No worries." She breathed a warm breath into her cupped hands then rubbed them together.

It's not like I'm on a winter break and this is one of the few days you'll see me until summer.

The cover displayed a half-naked woman whose bronze skin, sculpted breasts, and thin form were traits far more gorgeous than Alice could ever hope for.

Alice admitted it to herself. *There will always be women prettier than me. I'll always be plain.*

Jack snapped the book shut and stood with a delicious, winning smile. "Hi, Beautiful." He frowned. "Why aren't you wearing your coat and boots?"

"Barbara blocked the doorway. I couldn't get to my coat and boots, so I had to use the back door."

Jack scowled. "Did she see you?"

Alice shook her head and grinned. "I'm as stealth as a sarpion."

"What's a sarpion?"

Alice whispered, "They're extremely stealthy creatures. You've never seen one, have you?"

"No."

"See?"

He laughed and kissed her, tracing her lips with his tongue. She kissed him back, taking in his sweet taste. Her insides wilted. This was the man she knew and loved.

"Guess what day it is today," Alice gazed up into his beautiful blue eyes.

"Wednesday?"

Alice chuckled away her disappointment. "It's the one-year anniversary of when we started seeing each other."

"That's right. You fell and knocked your head, and somehow that was just what we needed to bring us together. Let me put this book away and I'll get ready for bed."

"Okay." Alice warmed at the thought of cuddling with him.

Jack stepped past her to his bookshelf. Alice studied the toy ring on her finger, the one Jack had won for her at the county fair last summer. Alice looked up, Jack was walking backwards admiring his bookshelf.

Then he stepped on her toe.

"Ow!" She hopped on one foot and rubbed the sore toe with one hand.

He spun around. "Oh, sorry. I didn't see you."

"It's all right." She didn't meet his eye. She didn't know what hurt worse, her toe or not being seen.

Jack kissed her cheek and stripped off his clothes. She sat on the bed and watched his thick torso, his muscular arms, and his tight butt. She rubbed her toe, but it didn't hurt anymore, not with all of *that* to look at.

Under the covers, they made love like they had every night since she'd been back from university. She lay underneath him and their love-making was nice. His thrusts felt good and he finished inside of her, the comfort of his solid body resting on top of her.

He rolled off of her and lay at her side. "Did you climax?" he panted.

"Almost."

He propped himself on his elbow. "I'm sorry, Alice. Here. Let me—"

"It's okay, Jack. It was lovely." Alice placed a hand on his cheek. "It's late. You better get some sleep. I know you need to be up early. You must be tired."

He sighed. "I am indeed."

"Go to sleep, Jack."

He nodded. "Okay. Sweet dreams, Alice." He kissed her lips, a quick delicate kiss.

"Goodnight, Jack." She turned away and let him spoon her, his arms around her chest, so near her disappointed heart.

2. Jack's Cottage

If you saw your true self,
Would you recognize her?

ALICE yawned awake in Jack's bed. She reached out for him. The cold sheets greeted her.

She was alone in Jack's cottage. Jack must have gone to work already, starting the fireplaces in her parents' manor. Though mainly a gardener, Jack had a variety of handyman duties both inside and outside the manor.

She checked the bedside clock. Strange. The clock hands were missing.

Alice examined the one-room cabin. Everything was tiny, as though designed for her cat Dinah to use.

A tiny chair with a tiny table where Jack used to serve her dinner and breakfast, and a tiny bookshelf with a few tiny books whose spines were too old and too small to be readable.

Alice yawned again, flipped the covers off her naked body, and tiptoed across the floor to the bathroom. Stroking back a lock of her blonde hair, she peered at herself in the large vanity mirror. Was she slouching? She tried pushing her shoulders back, thrusting out her breasts. She still looked like she was slouching. And one of her breasts looked smaller than the other. She'd seen that sort of thing before. Her sister Lois had breasts of slightly different sizes, but this was the first time Alice noticed it on herself.

More than her chest was off. One of her blue eyes was squinting. Or were they both squinting?

No, not exactly squinting. More like bunching up because of the grin forming at her lips.

Was she smiling? Alice put her fingertips to her mouth to check, but the reflection's arms didn't move. The mirror image of herself kept her hands at her side.

Lord, what was going on?

The reflection started laughing, harder and harder. The woman in the mirror held her belly, trembling with laughter, then wiped at her eyes.

The woman peered at her and spoke, "You look ridiculous. You do realize that, don't you?"

This wasn't happening. Couldn't be happening.

The woman reached beside her, grabbing something out of view of the mirror's frame. "Let me show you your true reflection." She returned, bucket in hand, filled with black goo. "See this?"

Was that a bucket of tar?

The woman poured some of the tar over her own head, the black goo spilling down her blonde hair and porcelain shoulders.

She shrugged. "This is what you are. Nothing. Just an insignificant mess to ignore." She sneered, "Nobody sees Alice anymore. Nobody sees you or cares about you."

"That's not true." Alice balled her hands into fists. "Jack cares about me. He cares about me a lot."

Right?

"Oh, he does, does he? And what makes you think so?" The shiny tar covering the woman's hair dripped to her shoulders.

Alice struggled to answer her but the words wouldn't come.

The black-haired woman curled her lips into a cruel smile. "No witty answer? Face it. Jack doesn't care about you. How do I know? Because he doesn't treat you well."

"Yes, he does." Alice's stomach fluttered with doubt and she wondered why she felt like she was lying to herself.

"Really? When was the last time he cooked for you? When was the last time he held your hand?

When was the last time he made love to you?"

Now here was a question Alice could respond to with confidence. "We made love last night."

The woman huffed. "I'm not talking about sex. You and Jack have issues. I don't think you have it in you to deal with it, so you and Jack will need to visit my Wonderland six times. After the sixth time, you will fully grasp who you are and what you need."

Alice scowled. What was she talking about?

Alice stared at this strange woman in the mirror. Mirror-Alice was a mess, the tar sticking to her skin and dripping down her bare shoulders.

The black-haired woman nodded her chin to Alice's hand. "That the ring Jack gave you?"

Alice held up her hand and admired the ring on her pinky. Jack had won the ring in a ball toss booth at the county fair.

He'd placed the small metal ring with its cute plastic pink jewel on Alice's pinky saying, "I know it's not worth millions, but it represents how much my heart cares for you."

He sealed his promise with a kiss.

She sighed at the memory. The ring meant more to her than any real jewelry her parents bought for her.

Alice gazed from her dear ring to the woman in the mirror. "What about it?"

"The ring will guide you," the woman nodded. Her voice sounded sincere, all the mocking gone from her voice. "When you take the proper path of your true needs and desires, and live your true connection, a reconnection with Jack, the ring will tell you. Now get the hell out of here!"

The woman threw the remaining tar at Alice. The mirror between them shattered into her face.

ALICE woke up to swat away glass and tar. But there was no glass and tar. Where was she? She blinked, her eyes adjusting to the early morning light. She was in Jack's bed, the place that witnessed Jack's love for her.

She shivered under the wool blanket, though Jack's body heat warmed her back. Her nightgown's thin fabric and blankets couldn't keep out the freezing mid-winter air in Jack's cabin.

Was Jack still asleep? The steady sound of his deep breaths gave away that he was.

Alice tightened the blankets around her and shivered.

She had just dreamed a dream. What was it? Something awful. Something just out of reach of her memory. She wanted to remember though.

Alice pressed her hands at her cheeks and gazed at her pinky ring, the ring Jack had given to her.

She remembered. A woman told her the ring would guide her.

What woman? A woman with long black hair.

No. It was worse than that. It was a woman in the mirror. Alice's own reflection.

Her reflection had told her the ring would guide her, that Jack didn't care about her, and that some six trips would help her discover who she was and what she needed.

No. More than that.

The ring would guide her to reconnect with Jack. Did she really need to reconnect?

The woman mocked her relationship with her beau.

It had been one year since she'd become Jack's girlfriend, but since Alice spent most of that year at university, they were supposed to be still in their honeymoon period, spending all day staring into each other's eyes.

It had started out that way. Jack cooked nearly every meal the first week. His gaze fixed on hers while they made love. When she came to see him he always had a smile for her. But lately, he didn't have time to make her special meals. He didn't jump to his feet to greet her when she visited his cabin. Worse, he seemed to stop looking at her when they made love. So where did his love go?

She twirled the light pinky ring.

Christmas was in six days. Were the six trips

referring to the six days from now until Christmas? Was that what the woman in the mirror meant?

Then what? Then Christmas, then back to Newnham, the all-girls college at Cambridge University.

Another thing about her dream flashed, that of the cabin all misshapen.

Alice glanced around the small cottage. The table and single chair was back to regular size. The bookshelf's classics clearly displayed their titles, unlike in her dream where they'd been unreadable. It gave her comfort to read the titles of her childhood classics: *The Three Musketeers*, *Treasure Island*, *Dracula*, and *Swiss Family Robinson*. She shivered when her eyes landed on the *She* title, and the memory of the perfect sculpted temptress on the cover.

A single door opposite the bed led to the compact bathroom. It had no vanity mirror like the one in her dream. She shivered at the weirdness of her dream and scanned the cabin for more ordinary items to bring her back to the real world.

Arching her back, Alice saw that on the wall behind her head, dangling from a nail, hung the pair of leather gloves she had given Jack as a gift on their third day together. She relaxed and spooned closer to Jack's warm, sleeping form, his rear cozy with her belly. Her desire for him flared.

They'd made love last night. No, that was sex,

not making love. Jack didn't look into her eyes anymore. He just stared at the wall above her head or closed his eyes.

Alice exhaled. This couldn't be the end of them. They could still make love.

In his sleep, Jack shifted to lie on his back.

Alice snuggled closer to his side.

I'm his girlfriend. He can still express his love for me.

She reached out to his bare chest, her fingertips lightly painting down his abdomen, feeling his muscles move with his every breath. A lick of his black hair draped over one eye. His thin lips parted enough to let his breath come easily. His chiseled chin and strong jaw made him seem commanding even in his unconscious state. Lord, he was handsome.

She painted her fingertips back up his chest and then down again, wanting him, needing him. Alice touched her breast and slipped the fingers of her other hand down his boxer shorts.

She gasped. He was already hard. This wasn't the first time she noticed him fully erect while asleep. The first time it had happened, she woke up feeling his cock against her bottom and thought he was trying to start something. When she turned around and found him still sleeping, she didn't understand how that was even possible. Was he having a sexy dream? Was it with her? When she later asked him about it, he chuckled and said it always happened and had nothing to do with dreams. Hard to believe, but Alice had taken his word for it.

Now he was hard again. Sure, he had been telling the truth when he said dreaming had nothing to do with his erection, but the question still popped into her mind.

Is he dreaming of me?

She gripped his length.

Jack is here, with me, with no one else. He loves me. He has to.

She stroked him imagining what his dream might be.

Are you dreaming of being my knight in shining armor, taking me on your horse, and taking me in your bed, lancing me to save me from myself? Are you dreaming of being my handsome prince, whisking me, your fairytale princess, away from the castle ballroom into the master bedroom to check if your shoe fits me?

Alice's breathing shallowed. She pinched her nipple with one hand and stroked him further.

His eyes fluttered toward consciousness.

Are you dreaming of being my Pinocchio, telling me lie after lie until I scream of ecstasy? Or are you dreaming of being my Peter Pan, taking me away to your Neverland, filling me with thimbles?

Alice tingled and dripped.

Jack shifted in bed, taking in a deep breath. He finally opened his eyes.

Alice squeezed his cock. He smiled sleepily.

"Make love to me," Alice whispered.

His gravelly voice rumbled. "Morning sex? Mmm. I'm a lucky guy."

Alice winced. She had asked for lovemaking, not sex.

"What's wrong?" Jack asked.

"Just," Alice said, "make love to me."

"Your wish is my command." He whisked off his boxer shorts

Her wish wasn't the same as his own wish? He felt she was commanding him? Was this a chore for him?

Jack levered himself above her. Alice spread her legs. The bed rocked unsteadily under their new positions. He licked his fingers and rubbed her clit, getting her wet enough for him like he always did. It meant putting much of his weight on his other hand, the hand that held him up.

The wooden planks of the bed creaked.

He guided himself into Alice, stretching her open to him. She let out a moan to let him know how good it felt. But did it truly feel as good as she portrayed? She tried not to think about it and reached for his back to invite more of him in. He inserted deeper.

Was this making love? Was this their relationship?

The bedsprings whined.

*****

JACK loved the feeling of being inside Alice, but couldn't shake the guilt. He had loved beautiful women before, but Alice was different. Maybe he should have felt good about that. Maybe he should have celebrated how he loved having Alice in his bed because of who she was.

But he enjoyed her for the wrong reason. He couldn't shake the idea that he was having sex with his employer's daughter. Damn, that made him feel bloody powerful.

"Jack, stay with me," Alice whispered.

Jack peered down at Alice's stunning face, her blonde curls framing her blue eyes, her soft skin, her supple lips. He continued pushing into her, watching how her body shifted with each thrust, relishing the power he commanded over her, Mr. Dellid's daughter, and how her eyes rolled backwards in pleasure because of him.

But loving her this way was wrong, wasn't it?

Jack slowed the pace to do the opposite of what his gut wanted. He wanted to pound her, make her writhe, watch her squirm in agonizing bliss, all to dominate her, Alice, his employer's daughter.

It was wrong. Jack knew he had to do the right thing, so he slowed down. Alice looked up at him and smiled.

Her eyes sparkled. "Isn't this lovely?"

"Yes," Jack replied. It was the right thing to say.

He planted his hands at her ankles and pushed into her. Something about holding her ankles felt amazing.

On the wall above Alice's head hung the leather gloves she had given him to keep warm during the winter work. He had hung them there on purpose.

His thoughts drifted to a recent fantasy. What would it be like to wear those gloves and press Alice against the wall facing him? To pin her by her wrists with one hand? To stuff two leather fingers up her pussy until she screamed out dripping orgasm after orgasm?

"Jack," Alice broke his fantasy. "Stay with me."

What did she mean by that? Did she think he was going to leave the bed?

"I'm not going anywhere." Jack pushed gently into her and the stimulation stirred him higher. He was getting close. He closed his eyes.

He pictured Alice in a red dress. What would it be like to wear those gloves and take her over his knees? To raise her dress and yank her panties down? To jam a couple of fingers in and out of her at ruthless speed until she cried out her sopping climax and begged for rest?

Opening his eyes to the gloves on the wall, he neared the edge and needed just that extra push to find release. He hammered away, watching his cock pound into her, into Mr. Dellid's daughter, into Alice.

A stream slipped through his cock. He clenched his final thrust into her. Another stream pulsed out. And another. Memories of every order Mr. Dellid had given him flowed through Jack and shot right into Mr. Dellid's daughter. Every command, every task, bottled and sprayed out of Jack. He sprayed inside Alice, filling employer's daughter with cum, impaling her on his cock, clamping down on her ankles and filling her until he was done.

He collapsed onto her, catching his breath. The thoughts had been wrong, but he couldn't help it. It had felt so good.

Oh, no.

No, no, no. Were those tears in her eyes?

Jack's gut sank. "What's wrong?"

"It's nothing," Alice smiled, drying her eyes.

That smile seemed forced. She was hiding something.

Alice looked away, at the clock. "It's late. You need to go help with starting the fires."

Damn. She was right.

Jack climbed out of bed and put on his wool shirt, overalls, work boots, and gloves.

Opening the front door, Jack turned to Alice. "Come find me during my afternoon break. We'll talk about it then, okay?"

Alice nodded. "Go."

Damn. Jack gently closed the door behind him.

3. The Hired Help and a Naughty Neighbor

When people meet you, do they meet your true self,
Or do they meet the one they expect you to be?

Alice couldn't believe it. She had asked him to love her and instead he screwed her. The love was gone.

She stepped to the bathroom, collected a bit of tissue paper, and wiped her eyes as the remnants of Jack's cum dripped down her thighs. She felt like his personal piss pot.

She blew her nose and moved to the cabin

window. The first snow was still falling. She used to get excited at the sight. Now it felt like a premonition of colder times to come.

Two of the recently hired helpers were out in the snow collecting firewood. One of the young men must have noticed he was being watched because he looked back at Alice, a grin forming on his face.

Why was he smiling?

Alice felt her chest warm up when she figured it out. Her nightgown must have been pleasing him. No, not the nightgown. What he saw underneath. The way the sheer fabric revealed the naked figure, the way the cold air set her nipples at full attention. It must have been quite a show.

She planted a hand on her hip, shifted to one leg, and smirked right back, daring him to keep gawking.

Though his voice was hard to hear through the window, she heard him call out to the other worker, "Hey, Billy! Take a gander at the bird over there."

The one named Billy raised his head from his wood-collecting and followed his friend's gaze to Alice.

"You'd be best to pay no mind." Billy averted his eyes. "That's Jack's mate."

That should have been flattering, right? But her body didn't seem to think so. A sinking pain dripped through Alice's chest.

Jack's mate? Was that the way people saw her now? She was losing herself. She didn't even have her own name anymore. Had she really been so blind? The woman in her dream was right. She wasn't Alice anymore. She was just Jack's mate. No one saw her for who she was.

The first worker's smile vanished and both of them returned to collecting firewood.

Alice stepped into the cold, stomping on the virgin snow. She welcomed the sting of the snow at her feet, and the chill biting her nipples through her thin nightgown. So what if the boys could see her figure? The veil of her nightgown felt like a veil of mourning, mourning the loss of who she once was.

What was she, after all? Just a vessel for Jack to fill? She didn't know what maddened her more, the way Jack took her for granted, or the way the boys visibly forced themselves not to look at her because she was "Jack's mate." Alice approached the manor's back door when she heard a nearby sound of footsteps crunching the snow.

"Thank you," a man's voice said.

She turned. It was Troy, her neighbor and childhood playmate. He carried a crate of milk bottles. As a helpful neighbor, he always picked up the milk for Alice's family from the milkman and carried it from the milkman's cart to Alice's manor.

She admired his dimpled smile. "Why do you thank me?"

"For forgetting to put on clothes before going out this morning." He poured his gaze from her head to her toes so thick she could feel it. Lord, was she getting wet just by his leer?

She put a hand on her hip and sneered. "Go ahead. Take it in. It'll be the last time you get to see me this close to naked. It'll probably be the last time you ever see a woman this close to naked."

"If you had any idea of how big I was, you'd change your tune pretty quickly and beg for it."

We'll see about that.

Alice imagined squeezing in a place behind her eyes. She could feel it, like two rocks inflating there, pushing against her eyes. Ever since she had fallen and hit her head last year, she discovered a strange new power. She could see through things. Sure it meant feeling pressure behind her eyes and generating a self-inflicted headache, but now seemed one of those rare moments she was willing to take on the pain. Just how big was Troy?

The first layer at Troy's clothing blurred and disappeared. His cock was cradled by a jock strap that seemed to only hold the bottom portion of his length. Lord! As she followed up the strap's supporting pouch to the bottom of his shirt, she saw his erection reaching past his belly button.

He adjusted his trousers. "You know, we should play another game of Simon Says. Like we did as kids."

Alice curled her toes at the idea. When they were younger, Simon Says led to a lot of clothes falling to the floor. He was the first boy she'd ever seen in underwear.

She shook her head. "I shouldn't be flirting with you. I have a boyfriend." But she was wet for him already.

"Are you happy?"

"Yes." Alice shrugged. So what, if she was lying.

"Then you're right. You shouldn't be flirting with me. I'll take you over my knee and give you a proper spanking for that."

Alice clenched her thighs. "I'd like it too much." Liking a spanking? True or not, she enjoyed the tease.

"I'll save all your punishments for when you break up with him. Then I'll give them to you all at once."

Alice smiled. "That's as likely to happen as you ever seeing me wear this nightgown again."

Before he could respond, she traipsed into the manor and filed that fantasy of punishments for another day.

Why doesn't Jack treat me that way? He used to treat me like a queen and now he treats me like a peasant. It's time to tell him.

Alice shivered at the idea of confronting him, but why was it so hard? He was a servant. The family always told him what to do, and Jack always listened. He especially listened to her father. Alice decided to talk to him the way her father talked to him.

*****

JACK thrust another log into the dining room fireplace. The fire recoiled at the new log, as though trying to determine what to do with it. Jack shivered. Why was Alice upset? The question nagged at him. He shook his head. He must have done something wrong. But what?

He knew there was a bigger question he was avoiding.

He wiped the remaining bark and dirt from his gloves on his trousers.

Whatever it was that he had done wrong, could she ever forgive him to stay together? Or was this the end? When a woman cries after sex, in his experience it was likely over something that could never be fixed.

"Jack?"

Jack whipped around.

"Alice." His heart pounded in his chest, as if she'd caught him with his hand in her forbidden cookie jar.

She stood with her arms crossed at the dining room doorway. She had changed out of her nightgown and wore her sleeveless yellow dress.

Jack waited for her to speak.

She's going to break up with me. I could tell her it's okay, not to worry about me. I'll be fine. But dammit I refuse to make this easy for her.

Alice took a deep breath. "I want to be treated as if I'm someone special to you. I want everyone to see me as someone special, not just 'Jack's mate.' " She gazed at the floor, as if the words lay at her feet. "I want to be treated like a queen."

Like a queen? Was she asking for jewelry and expensive gifts? "What do you mean?"

Alice huffed. "It bothers me that you don't give me what I need, but it bothers me even more that you don't know what I'm talking about."

Jack didn't understand. His wages hardly supported himself, much less a queen.

"Alice, I think I know what you're asking for." How could he tell her he didn't have enough money to give her all the things she wanted. "But I don't know that I can."

Her jaw dropped and her eyes welled. She ran upstairs.

Jack rushed after her.

Making such a firm demand was so unlike Alice. It was as if a different person said those words. He never saw that coming.

By the time he got to her bedroom, she had already slammed the door shut. He tried the knob. Locked. He had the key to all the manor's rooms, including the bedrooms, but he would never be so improper as to enter a room without permission.

"Alice, open up."

No answer.

"You're going to have to let me in soon. I still have to water the plants in your room."

"Leave me alone." Her sobbing rushed at him, a punch in the gut.

"Alice, please open the door."

No answer.

What could he do? He had to talk to her. "Alice?"

No answer.

Bloody hell. Jack took out the keys to the manor, got poised to insert her key into the keyhole, then paused. He weighed the ring of keys in his hand—the trust Mr. Dellid had placed in him—and decided. No. He had to respect her choices.

Jack pocketed the keys and knocked. "Come on, Alice."

No answer.

There was nothing Jack could do to calm her down. At least, not with enough time left to finish building the fires in the rest of the manor's fireplaces. In truth, he didn't know what he could say to make her happy. He stomped down the staircase to attend to the stubborn dining room fireplace.

She had to know that he couldn't afford to buy her luxuries. And hadn't she said that she didn't care about his social status?

He knelt at the fireplace.

Maybe she changed her mind. Maybe she saw now that she needed a wealthy gentleman to grace her with gifts and expensive baubles.

Jack grabbed a piece of a branch and shoved it into the fire. The branch resisted. A splintered piece of it pierced through the glove and punctured his palm. He hissed at the stinging pain and yanked off the glove to suck on the wound. His mind filled with curses as the metallic taste of blood spread across his tongue.

4. The Library

Even the smallest room, when filled with books,
Is one where you can become lost.

ALICE knew Jack would have to water her plants eventually. The only way to avoid him further was to escape to the library.

She scooped up her tabby cat Dinah and padded to the toasty library. Jack had already lit the fire in this room, so Alice knew he wouldn't return. He had other fires to start. She could be alone, burning away her tears.

What was she going to do? What *could* she do? If

he didn't love her anymore, she couldn't change his mind. She had no control over how Jack felt about her. If he did still love her, he didn't show it. Even telling him what she wanted wasn't enough. What was left?

Helplessness dug a hole into her stomach.

She shut the library door and puffed out a breath. The library seemed the proper place for her to be. The room held books that begged for attention, just like her.

A gold gilded hand mirror lay beside a chessboard on the long oak reading table. She picked up the mirror. Her reflection didn't impress her. Her face was fat. What was there to love?

She dropped the mirror on the table with a clatter.

No wonder Jack doesn't love me. I'm just something to slam his cock into.

Alice yelled out an angry cry. With a sweep of her hand, she brushed the chessboard off the table. The chess pieces tumbled and scattered across the carpeted floor, not making a satisfying bang as she'd hoped.

Dinah mewed, a worried expression on her feline face. At least, Alice thought it was worry. Hard to tell with cats.

Alice collapsed to the rug and pet Dinah. The cat arched its back meeting Alice's loving strokes.

"You're lucky, Dinah. You're too cute to be

ignored. What is it about your magical purr that makes us want to treat you like a queen?"

Alice scratched Dinah behind the ears. Dinah purred louder.

"You're not the only one who's lucky," Alice said. "Lois has her girlfriend Carol to dote on her. Mother has Father. Why, even the Snow seems to dote on its lover, the Earth. But Jack?"

Alice glared at the ring on her pinky. "Who am I kidding? I'm just not the right girl for Jack." She twirled the ring. "The sooner we break up, the less heartache there will be. Then we can move on." Her vision blurred wet.

She tugged the ring off her finger and gripped it in the palm of her hand. It wasn't just a ring. It was a symbol of Jack's love for her, a promise for their future together, filled with happiness, intimacy, and fulfillment.

Now it was a broken promise, full of lies, sorrow, and a cheap piece of metal.

She threw the thing across the library, stood, and took a deep breath.

It was time to end it with Jack. The sooner, the better. Knowing what to do felt good. Like she had her power back.

She turned toward the door, but just then, Carol, her sister's girlfriend, stepped in.

"Oh hi, Alice. Just the person I wanted to see." She smiled brightly, gazing about the book-lined library. She settled on Alice and continued. "Does your family have the book—What's wrong?"

"It's nothing." Alice shrugged and stepped toward the doorway.

Carol blocked her with a playful grimace, crossing her arms across her chest, as if she were pretending to be a guard. "Nuh uh. I'm not letting you leave until you tell me what's wrong."

"Carol, I'm not in the mood to play games." Alice glared at her.

But Carol seemed to see past her tough façade for she shook her head and took Alice by the hand. She closed the library door and led Alice to the table.

"Alice, sit down and tell me what's going on."

Alice sighed. Her shoulders sagged. She scooped up Dinah, and plopped in a plush chair by the couch. Dinah settled into her lap and took up her happy purr.

Carol sat opposite Alice in another plush chair and waited.

Alice sighed finally. "Jack doesn't love me anymore."

Carol gasped. "He told you that?"

"No, but by the way he's been treating me, I can tell."

Carol squinted. "What do you mean? How has he been treating you?"

Alice groaned. "It's not that. He doesn't hit me."

Carol scowled like she still didn't understand. Then her eyes widened and she grinned. "So you *want* him to hit you? Like a good spanking?"

"Carol!" What was it with everybody talking about spanking her?

She held up her hands in surrender. "I know, I know. My mind tends to go places better off censored. So what has Jack been doing that makes you think he doesn't love you? Has he been sleeping around?"

"No, it's just," Alice gave Dinah some loving pets, "I want to be treated like a queen. He doesn't treat me that way."

"You told him you wish to be treated like a queen?"

"Yes."

"Did you explain what you meant by that?"

"Well, no, but isn't it obvious?"

Carol laughed. "Alice, you give men more credit than they deserve." She chuckled and shook her head. Carol cleared her throat and fanned her face as if waving away her amusement. "Start by telling *me* what specifically you want."

Alice pet soft Dinah, sinking into her cat's purr to search for her words. How could she put this? "Jack doesn't give me the same attention he used to. He no longer cooks for me or brings home flowers from the garden."

"Oh, Alice." Carol smiled kindly. "That happens

in every relationship. When I first went out with your sister, I couldn't let her out of my sights. I wanted to spend every minute with her. But now we're more comfortable with each other, and just because I don't hold hands with her all the time doesn't mean I no longer love her."

Alice shook her head. "It's more than that." She shrugged. "When we're in bed together..." Alice didn't know how to word it.

Carol leaned in. "Yes?"

Alice let out a nervous smile. "When we're in bed together, it's like I'm not there. Even when we're doing, you know..."

"It feels like he's screwing you instead of making love?"

Alice exhaled in relief for not having to say it. "Exactly."

"And that hurts like hell."

Alice's throat filled with the saddest of sands. She choked them down, nodding.

Carol leaned back in her chair and tapped the armrest lost in thought.

Sadness embraced Alice even while she felt validated. It was okay to feel bad, to feel like a victim.

Carol scowled at Alice's hand. "Your pinky."

"What about it?"

"Where's the ring Jack gave you?"

Alice motioned to the bookshelves. "I was angry, so I took it off and threw it over there somewhere."

"Alice," Carol scolded. She retrieved the ring and sat down. "A lot of men are jerks. They'll say they love you and that you're the most beautiful woman in the world, and then once you sleep with them they'll stop talking to you like you're not worth their time. Men can be cruel assholes." She took Alice's hand. "But Jack isn't one of them. He loves you. I can tell. You are not breaking up with Jack."

Carol slid the ring back on Alice's pinky. All the promises of Jack's love came flooding back.

"I don't know if I can go through this again," Alice said. "Jack might just continue to ignore me."

"Alice, do you feel like a queen?"

"No."

"Then how do you expect to be treated like one?" Carol shook her head. "Have you heard the story of 'The Eight-Horse Woman?' "

"No."

"There were two men sailing across the rough, choppy seas, Nathaniel and… Bob."

Alice smirked. "Bob?"

"I don't remember. It doesn't matter. So the boat gets torn apart by the storm and Nathaniel and Bob get lost and end up on a remote island. They walk a few miles and discover a tribe celebrating the coronation of their new queen. Both Nathaniel and Bob are stunned by the queen's beauty. They ask the nearby rancher about the queen. The rancher invites them over to teach them about his tribe."

"A rancher lives with a tribe?"

"It's my story, Alice. I can tell it however I want." Carol smiled. "As they sit themselves at the rancher's table, the rancher's daughter Solette serves them dinner. Nathaniel takes one look at Solette and says, 'Damn, you're beautiful!' Bob and the rancher are rather confused by Nathaniel's comment. To Bob, the woman is covered with grime, slouches, can't make eye contact, and is an overall homely gal. But Nathaniel gets on his knees and asks her to marry him. She drops the food she was carrying and runs to the kitchen."

"Was he serious when he asked her to marry him?"

"Don't get ahead of me, Ms. Jiffy." Carol smoothed out her dress. "So Nathaniel apologizes to the rancher for frightening his daughter. The rancher shrugs it off and asks, 'I have the same question as Alice. Are you serious about wanting to marry my daughter?' "

Alice smirked.

"Nathaniel wags his head yes. The rancher explains that the tradition is to pay a dowry of a horse to the father of the bride. Nathaniel asks, 'Is that the common dowry for the most stunning women of the tribe?' The rancher says, 'No, the most stunning women of the tribe, like the queen, requires a dowry of eight horses.' 'I will pay you eight horses,'

Nathaniel says. Bob is shocked and the rancher says, 'I was going to accept a chicken, but if you wish to give me eight horses, I won't object.' That settled, Nathaniel starts a job to raise enough money to buy eight horses and in the meantime visits Solette, giving her gifts. Bob repairs the sailboat and leaves the island."

Alice leaned in, curious to hear the rest of the story.

"Ten years later, Bob returns on a ship to visit his old friend Nathaniel. When he arrives, there is a huge celebration for the new queen of the tribe just like the first time he arrived. This queen is stunning, more beautiful than the first. I mean, she's absolutely radiant, glowing with pride and strength. Bob runs into Nathaniel in the crowd and together they catch up. Bob says how beautiful the new queen is. Nathaniel says, 'That's my wife.' Bob says, 'Really? Lucky man! So you decided not to marry that rancher's daughter after all, eh?' Nathaniel shakes his head. 'You don't understand. That beautiful queen is Solette, the rancher's daughter.' Bob's jaw drops. 'The one we met when we first arrived?' Nathaniel nods. 'The very same.' Bob can't believe it. 'How is that possible? She was rather ugly back then, and now she looks amazing.' Nathaniel claps Bob on the shoulder. 'If you treat a woman like an eight-horse woman, she'll believe she's an eight-horse woman. And if she believes she's an eight-horse woman, everyone else will believe it, too.' "

Alice shivered. Carol's message was clear.

Carol adjusted her dress. "Jack may not treat you like a queen, but if you believe you're a queen, an eight-horse woman, then Jack will see that and treat you that way."

Alice rubbed at the goose bumps fluttering up her arms. "I think it's one of those things where convincing myself that I deserve to be adored is easier said than done."

Carol nodded. "It may take a bit of time, but you'll get there eventually."

Helplessness buried itself in Alice's gut. "What should I do?"

Carol shook her head. "Maybe think about what you're good at and focus on doing those things. That might give you the confidence you need to show Jack how deserving you are of his undivided attention."

Alice said nothing.

"You're an amazing woman, Alice. Believe in yourself. Believe you are the queen that I know you to be, and get clear on what that means so you can explain it to Jack." Carol stood. "And if that doesn't work, you can always try a blowjob. I need to find Lois. Come let me give you a hug."

Alice's nervousness came out in a laugh. She stood, and hugged Carol. "Thank you," she whispered.

Carol whispered back, "Find your confidence. Become a queen." She let go of Alice and padded out of the library.

Alice sighed and eyed the library's couch that lay beside the window. Perfect for a nap and to slip away from all the morning's drama.

JACK shook his head and glared at the low fire as if it held the answers. He didn't understand her. Alice had always done some crazy things but usually out of playfulness.

Jack remembered how he enjoyed her antics before they were lovers. During the summer before she had to leave for university, she'd visited his cabin one afternoon holding a copper weathervane and a cardboard cutout of an ax.

Jack had been amused and prepared himself for whatever performance Alice had in store for him.

"To what do I owe the pleasure?" He smiled at her odd props.

"When you were helping Barbara in the kitchen last night, I overheard you tell her how you have a lot of gnats near your cabin, so I brought you some weapons to defend yourself against them."

Jack chuckled. "I see." He sat down on his bed. "Please. Continue."

Alice set down the weathervane on his table and held up the cutout of the ax. "This is called a 'battle Jacks.' You can use it to strike down those nasty bloodsuckers."

She demonstrated, swinging the cardboard cutout through the air, accompanied by what Jack could only guess were battle cries. "Hyah! Hyah!"

Jack laughed and nodded at the weathervane on the table. "Is that also supposed to be a weapon?"

Alice set the ax on the table and picked up the copper cutout shaped like an arrow with a rooster perched on top. "This is what will distract the gnats as you hack them to pieces. Once they get inside your cabin, they'll pass right by you and go straight to this 'Jackular vein.'"

Jack laughed as Alice handed him the vane. "Thank you, Alice. You're lucky. The manor isn't as close to the water as my cabin is. You don't get as many gnats."

"That's not true. We have them all the time. Why, just last night I got bitten by one of those things and got a huge red bump on my shin. Take a look."

She turned, showing off her profile and bent over, sliding up the hem of her pink dress. She exposed her outer shin, but there was no red bump there.

"I think it's higher up." Alice slowly raised her

skirt higher, revealing her creamy white thigh.

Jack's heart rate increased. Getting aroused by this was ridiculous because he had seen Alice in shorts many times. She was trying to get him worked up on purpose.

He masked a smile. Perhaps her intention turned him on more than her physical features.

"Not there," she said. "I think it's higher up."

Centimeter by excruciating centimeter, she hiked the skirt higher, her naked hip setting off all sorts of whistles and alarms in Jack's cock. He thanked his lucky stars that he was sitting. Sitting made it easier to hide his growing excitement she caused by her play.

Jack swallowed. Maybe her intention to arouse him was responsible for getting his heart racing, but that long length of alabaster leg sure helped.

It wasn't until he had eyed her nakedness up and down a few times that he realized she was watching him with a wicked grin.

Caught, Jack scratched the back of his itching neck.

She dropped the hem of her dress like a curtain closing on an amazing show. "Now I remember. The gnat bit me on the shoulder, not the leg."

Alice faced him and tugged on her short sleeve, sliding it at that same slow rate off her shoulder. Her eyes stayed locked on his own.

Maybe her intention was to get him excited, but

Jack could tell by the form-fitting top of her dress that her own breathing was getting heavier. He wasn't the only one enjoying this.

She didn't even turn to check her shoulder when she said, "Not there. I think it's further down."

She pulled the sleeve further, the neckline of her dress exposing more cleavage. Just as she got to that critical zone of possible over-exposure, she stretched her neckline outward and peeked down the front of her dress at her breast. She smiled.

"There it is. It's all red and swollen." She looked at Jack with innocent seriousness. "Would you like to see?"

Jack controlled his desire to jump at her, yank down her top, suck that nipple and give it a nibble just for good measure to add realism to her story.

Instead, he stood, hoping she wouldn't see how hard he was, and stepped to the door. "Okay, Alice. I think you should go."

"Fine." She shrugged her shoulder back into the short sleeve. "I'll see you again during winter break when I come home from university." She opened the door to leave. "Oh, and Jack?"

"Yeah?"

She grabbed him by the collar, a hand on either side of his face. She eyed him—his face, his chest—as though drinking him in.

Jack wanted to kiss her, but he knew that could get him fired. He pretended to disapprove of her behavior by raising an eyebrow at her.

She whispered in a husky voice, "You go get those gnats, Jack," and spun on her heel, marching away from the cabin.

The next day, Alice left for university. Jack didn't have room in his cabin to keep the weathervane, but he had kept the cardboard ax a few months until the rain came and a small flood in his cabin destroyed the souvenir. He had tried to dry it out, but the poor state of the battle Jacks, along with the memory it represented for him, was beyond saving. So Jack had let go of it, expecting both Alice and himself to move on. Thankfully when she returned from university to visit during winter break last year, she hadn't moved on, and neither had he. They became lovers.

Now Alice wanted to be with someone who could treat her like a queen and give her all the luxuries a wealthy man could offer. Such a relationship was no place for Jack.

His gut twisted at the thought of losing Alice. But the relationship was not about what made him happy, it was about what made them both happy. And if she wasn't happy being with him, then it wasn't really a relationship worth keeping.

Jack poked at the fire, stirring up sparks.

Maybe this whole queen thing was just her passive, indirect way of breaking up.

Jack nodded. Alice could never break up with him

directly. She was too nice of a person. So it was up to him. Jack figured the sooner the better.

He stabbed the fire one last time as though preparing for what he was about to do to his own heart.

ALICE stepped beside the bookshelves and absentmindedly traced the books with her fingertips. She skimmed across dictionaries, encyclopedias, a thesaurus and atlas, collected works of Shakespeare and Edgar Allen Poe and Homer, and books of quotations and sayings. The binding of the old books brought a gentle vibration up her arm. She stopped when she found an encyclopedia of famous people. She flipped through the listings to see what was it they were so good at to make them worthy of mention in the fat tome. Musty pages tickled her nose. There were engineers and leaders, scientists and philosophers, writers and artists, and even theologians.

She slammed the book shut. What was she expecting to find? People known for their skills at petting cats?

She shelved the encyclopedia and looked down at herself. Brushing her blonde hair off her shoulders, she would have admired her ample breasts, but the scoop neckline didn't do much to show them off. She sat at the library table. The hand mirror lay on the table, so she picked it up, held it high, and peered at herself.

There was nothing new to see. The same chubby-faced blonde-haired girl she saw everyday in the mirror. Not very queen-like.

"What skills do you have? Who are you?" she mused aloud.

Alice imagined squeezing pressure behind her eyes, focusing beyond the mirror. Her head spiked in pain. The mirror's glass and silver peeled away and revealed the books on the shelf directly behind the mirror.

"I suppose that's one talent I have that no one else has. But what does it get me? Just a peek at Troy's cock. I don't dare tell anyone about this supposed skill."

She relaxed her eyes and saw her face once more in the mirror.

What if she were to see inside herself?

Alice imagined those two rocks again, inflating behind her eyes, letting her head split with pain once more. This time, instead of focusing on the mirror, she focused on her image in the mirror and what she might see beyond the face.

"Who am I? Where is the queen inside Alice?"

Dizziness filled her head making it spin.

Clenching the mirror, she collapsed to the floor into the blackness.

5. Inside the Mirror

When you see your true self,
Careful not to shatter your image.

W HEN Alice awoke, she lay on the floor of the library, the sunlight rising through the window.

It's still morning? That's good. What happened?

She stared at the ceiling. A pain throbbed through her forehead. She rubbed her eyes and massaged her brow. The pain dwindled away.

Something was wrong with the library. She stood and scrutinized the books lined on the shelves. Their titles were backwards. Not just the titles, everything about the room was backwards. The position of the chairs, the reading table, the couch, the paintings—all were backwards.

The portrait of the captain showed him facing the bookshelves, not the windows as he always had before. The backwards portrait of the captain in the painting made Alice shiver, looking so very eerie. Something about his eyes.

Alice moved to the left, then to the right. No matter where she moved to in the room, the man's eyes avoided her. There was no spot in the room where the man seemed to look at her.

Alice sighed. "Even the paintings are ignoring me."

JACK climbed the stairs, his heart as heavy as clay soil. He was not looking forward to breaking up with Alice, but ending their relationship was the only way he could give her what she wanted. She wanted to be with someone who could give her expensive gifts, not just baubles and good intentions.

Halfway up the stairway, he passed Carol.

She smiled in her open and friendly way, with a hint of mischief in her gaze. "Alice said she wants to talk to you. She's in the library."

"Thanks." Jack nodded and continued on, not

wanting Carol to see his dark mood. He marched to the library door. His determination faltered and paused on the threshold. The door was open to the quiet room. He took a deep breath, then stepped in.

No one was there. Relief mixed with the disappointment that Alice was nowhere to be seen.

He turned to leave when he heard Alice's voice faint, as if from far away. He couldn't make out her words.

"Alice? Where are you?" He spun in a circle on the rug.

"Jack, I'm right here." Her voice came louder.

He frowned and peered under the table, but she wasn't there.

"Hey, I'm right here in the middle of the room," she huffed.

He spun again and frowned. "I don't see you. The only thing in the middle of the room is a mirror on the floor." He picked up the hand mirror. "Keep talking so I can follow the sound of your voice."

"I am here. I am here. I am here." She spoke quickly. "Follow my voice, follow my voice, la, la, la, la, la."

Jack couldn't help smiling. He bent at the waist and let his ear lead the way. The voice seemed to move as he did. Then he realized why. The mirror. Alice's voice came from the mirror.

He peered directly into it.

Alice stood in the center waving at him.

Bloody hell! "How is this possible? I see you through the mirror as if I'm looking through a window and you're standing right in front of me in the library. I can't even see *myself* in the mirror!"

She wrinkled her brow with worry. "Can you help me out of here?"

"How did you get there in the first place?"

Alice sighed. "Do you remember last year when I fell and hit my head?"

"That was the same day as our first night together. Of course I remember."

"Well, ever since then I've been able to see through things."

"Uh, explain."

"If I focus just right, I can see through objects." Alice explained how she first looked through the mirror but saw the opposite wall instead of herself. Then she looked for own image and got stuck inside the mirror world.

What Alice was reciting had to be nonsense, but what mattered was she believed it. And since Jack was witnessing what should have been impossible, maybe there was something to what she said.

"Hang on, Alice. I'll be right back."

He set the mirror on the table, ran down the hall to the nearest bathroom, and scoured the drawers for another hand-held mirror. He breathed a little easier when he found one. He ran back the library, picked up the first mirror, and sought out Alice. Inside the mirror, Alice stood, twirling her blonde curls and biting her lip.

"Okay, Alice. Let's try something. I'm going to hold up another mirror for you to look at and see if you can see through your reflected image in that one. Maybe that can bring you back."

Alice straightened her posture. "Very well."

Jack held up the second hand mirror. "Do you see your reflection?"

She scowled, then nodded.

"Go ahead and do whatever it was you did before."

Jack watched with a dropped jaw as all the colors of the rainbow beamed from Alice's mirror across to the second mirror. Slowly, Alice's body took its shape right in front of him, but the skin and muscles faded away leaving only skeleton. Jack's gut tightened. Soon the bones were also gone.

"Alice!" He yelled and peered through the first mirror. She was still there, but holding her head in her hands. "Alice, are you alright?"

"I'm fine. I just have a bit of a headache."

How could he get Alice out of that world? He had no bright ideas. Then he thought of something.

"Alice, why don't you try seeing what's outside the room?"

"Which way should I go? Should I try the door to the hallway, the playroom, or the deck?"

"Whichever."

Alice nodded and Jack steered the mirror to follow her as she walked away from the center of the library. Jack exhaled, almost relieved this bizarre problem occurred. It gave him a reason not to break up with her.

For now.

6. Escaping the Mirror

The more you hide from who you truly are,
The bigger the crash when your true self
Comes shattering out.

ALICE wrung her hands together. She thought it strange that Jack had to look through the mirror to see her. From her perspective, he was standing in the center of the room in his red and black plaid shirt and his olive-green overalls, and she could see him just fine without having to look through anything.

Alice opened the door that led to the playroom. At least, it should have led to the playroom. But all she saw was a library. Not just any library, the same library she was already in. In fact, across the room her own self faced away from her, looking out the opposite door.

She waved her hand and saw her own figure opposite her waving the same right hand. Was that what she looked like from behind? She frowned at the unfamiliar view.

Alice shook off the thought. She should be worried about getting out of this mirror world. What if she never got back? What if she were stuck here for the rest of her life?

She eyed the library. By simply having everything in reverse, the room looked fresh and new. She had to admit. This world was stunning.

Alice shivered. Spending the rest of her life here would be dreadful. But spending the day here? Even a week or month here could be an incredible vacation of sorts.

She stared at her backside. She admired her waist-long golden hair. She bunched her lemon yellow dress around her thighs and smiled at the nice, plump shape of her bum.

An identical Jack stood in the center of the other library, peering through the mirror and moving about as if lost. He then honed in on the same Alice she had her eyes on. What did *he* think of her backside?

"Jack, you're never going to believe this."

Both Jacks replied in unison. "What's wrong?"

"I can see myself. Look at the opposite door, the one to the deck."

Jack spun the mirror to the opposite side of the room.

She waved. "Do you see me?"

He looked back and forth between the two doors. "How are you in both places at once?"

"I don't know, Jack. Am I really here at all?" Alice snapped her fingers. "I must be dreaming." She returned to the first Jack at the center of the room and let him see her through the mirror. "It's alright. I'm just having a very vivid dream. All I need to do is wake up and I'll be out of this mirror land."

"I hate to say this, but if you're dreaming, then you're suggesting I'm not really here."

"That's right. You're not really here."

"Thanks a lot." His sarcasm sure sounded real.

"I'm sorry, Jack. It's just that since I'm dreaming... Wait a moment, why am I apologizing? You're not really here."

Jack huffed. "Very well. If you think you're dreaming, let's see you wake up."

"All right, then." Alice thought about it. If she jumped out the window, the jarred landing might pop her awake in her bed. But that was extreme. Even thinking about it hurt too much. Perhaps a good pinch was all it took.

She reached to pinch her arm, but stopped herself. "No."

"No, what?" asked Jack.

Miss out on this once-in-a-lifetime vacation? "No, I will not wake myself up. Why should I? If I'm dreaming, I can do whatever I want."

"Alice, this is serious. We've got to get you out of there."

She ignored him. If she wasn't going to be treated like a queen in reality, she could be treated like a queen in her dreams.

The more Alice thought about it, the more her heart raced, excited at the idea. Getting used to being treated like a queen could help her when she woke up. She could take that knowledge with her and know what it's like to be an eight-horse woman. Carrying herself with that much confidence would get back Jack's attention.

Alice eyed her surroundings and drank in her possibilities. She could manifest any fantasy she desired. Here, Jack stood in front of her and he would obey her command. What should she start with? Though she never had anal sex in reality, she had plenty of it the last time she dreamed of being in a strange wonderland. From what she remembered, it felt fantastic. She wanted to share that amazing experience with Jack.

"Take off your shirt."

"What?"

"You'll love this. I want you inside my ass, but first take off your shirt."

"Alice, you're being ridiculous. We have to find a way to get you out of this mirror."

Why wasn't he obeying her? This was *her* dream, shouldn't all the players do what she wanted? "If that's the way you feel about it, you can leave. This is my dream, I'm going to enjoy it as much as I can. I'd like to experience my fantasies with you, but if you're not interested, I'll just get someone else to do it."

He raised his voice. "Like who?"

"Like one of the boys outside, or Troy." She regretted saying the words as soon as they spilled from her lips.

Jack gasped. "Troy?"

His face reddened with anger. Alice worked at convincing herself this wasn't the real Jack, so she need not feel remorse for the way she spoke to him. Her cracking heart had trouble believing her own excuses.

Should I apologize? Alice felt the urge, even if this was just a dream. *No. A queen doesn't apologize. If I want to feel like a queen, I must act like one.*

Jack shook his head. "Alice, I can't do this."

"Do what?"

"I just—"

He grit his teeth and flung the mirrors at a bookshelf. They struck the shelf making Alice jump, and each landed on the carpet with a thud.

"You do what you want." Jack stormed out of the

room.

Alice's belly felt rancid and turned. None of this was real, she reminded herself. She took a deep breath to blow out the guilt. It helped, but not by much.

"Time to go exploring. Let's start with the library," she said to no one in particular, unless she counted the back of herself.

She peered at the shelves. She pulled out a blue leather-bound book and read the full title. It read "AHA" and the subtitle read "TIAW YHW."

It took Alice a moment to realize that the words were backwards. The book really said, "Aha, Why Wait." She opened the book to a middle page. There was an illustration of a man grinning over a woman's shoulder. Her dress was bunched up over her bum and his trousers were down to his ankles. The woman's eyes were squeezed shut and her lips pursed. Alice couldn't tell if the woman was experiencing pain or pleasure, nor where exactly the gentleman penetrated. She could see that he had a hand on the lady's shoulder and another hand clenching her breast.

On the opposite page was a poem, all in backwards script.

Alice set the open book on the table, picked up one of the hand mirrors Jack threw, and read the poem through the mirror.

THE SALICIOUS ONE

'Twas fair, a lady, red hair a-smolder,
Curves of nineteen, and not a curve older.
Three Yingish men came, Brass, Brazen, and Buck.
Brass fed her warnings with phallical huck.

"Beware the Salicious One, lady of lage,
His fing'rings and lickings he wickingly lays."
"Whate'er do you mean?" asked Red Hair a-smolder.
"I'll demonstrate," Brazen smirked gripping her
shoulders.

He shuppled her lips right up against his,
Kissing the singe, a light to her nips.
His fingers, they found twixt her legs her unknowing,
And taught her the danger of Salicious One's
stroking.

The woman she wilted with slick wisdom dripping,
But not good enough was this bodice a-ripping.
Hands on his hips, strong Buck steppered in,
"Beware the Salicious One's cruel staff of skin."

He revealed the likes of the waistful threat,
And bent her over the Tickling Tree's bret.
With a one and a two and a snickery snack,
The lady a-trembling came thrustering back.

The lass she did turn the color of pleasure.
"Lessons like these, I surely shall treasure."
And when all three filled her with lessons of depth,

She brushed down her dresses and straightened her breath.

Today if you see lady Red Hair a-smolder,
Curves of nineteen and not a curve older,
You'll see a woman well-versed in reason,
On how to avoid the Salicious One's treason.

She shows all her Yingish men how she avoids him,
Until they are spent in the glow of her wisdom.
Such studies you'll learn in each dreamicatesson.
And now, dear Alice, it's time for your lesson.

Alice gasped upon reading the words directed at her.

She shook it off. If this was her dream, then of course all that she saw would speak directly to her.

She clenched her thighs. She was going to enjoy this dream.

A scuffling came from below. Then a voice.

"I must write my memos," the voice bellowed.

Alice peered down. Many chess pieces rolled on the floor as if struggling to stand upright. The white king stood and held a pencil much too big for his tiny arms.

"Memo: I must help my chess pieces stand." He struggled with writing the words on a pad of paper.

What was a pad of paper doing on the floor?

Alice shrugged. What was a chess piece doing writing memos, for that matter? It was just a dream.

The king struggled to get a better hold of the pencil. "And now for my next memo. What else must I remember to do?"

Alice smiled and pinched the top of the pencil, prepared to force the king to write different words. She giggled without making much noise.

The king pressed the pencil to the pad of paper and spoke out the words as he wrote. "I must... remember... to read... my memos."

He checked his work. "That's odd. It says 'I must dismember my ready nose.' Let me try again. I must..." (scribble, scribble) "remember to read..." (scribble, scribble) "my memos." He checked his work. "Strange. Now it says, 'I dust my member to seed my clothes.' "

The king tried a third time. "I must remember to read my memos." Alice kept control of his pencil. He checked his work. " 'When drinking soda pop, never burp through your nose.' I wrote no such thing!"

Alice clapped her hand over her mouth to make sure the king wouldn't hear her giggles.

The king frowned. "I say, it's very disturbing to think one thing and write another. If only I had my queen, then she could help me understand what I'm doing wrong."

Alice gasped. She had an idea. There must be a way to become an actual queen in this dream.

She had told Jack she wanted to be treated like a queen, but as Carol had pointed out, Alice didn't exactly say what treating her like a queen meant. She needed to tell him, and it would be so much easier if she had the confidence. By becoming a legitimate queen in this dream, she could see what it was like to have the confidence and charisma she needed to face Jack. She could become an eight-horse woman.

But she'd have to hurry. If she woke up before becoming queen, she might never know how to be an eight-horse woman. She might come across as just a nagging chore and say the wrong thing to Jack, and Jack would break up with her. She had to get as small as the size of the chess pieces and become their queen.

All she needed was some cake or mushrooms to change her size.

7. Escaping the Library

Do you explore beyond your boundaries?
Or do you trap yourself to stay safe
Within your walls of comfort?

ALICE searched the bookshelves, chairs, and sofa. There was no sign of any cake or mushroom that said, "eat me." How was she going to make herself as small as the—

Looking at the floor, Alice saw that the king had disappeared. All the chess pieces were gone. She shivered and huddled closer to the warmth of the fire in the fireplace. But it didn't feel very warm. In fact, the flames felt rather cold. Where had the chess pieces gone?

Alice peered outside the window. There they were. The chess pieces were strutting down a dirt path. The bishops, the knights, the rooks, and the pawns marched two by two, all led by the king without his queen.

The chess pieces have gone outside and they're leaving. I have to get out of this room to catch up with them. I have to connect with the king and explain to him my situation. I must be their queen.

What were her options to escape the library?

Jack had left through the hallway door, that was one option. Then there were the side doors. One led to the playroom and the other led to the deck. But when Alice had opened the door to the playroom, it had just led to another library. If the door to the deck just led to another copy of the library, as the playroom door had, then neither of those doors worked as a feasible way to get out and explore the rest of this wonderland.

"Jack left this way." She twisted the hallway doorknob.

The door flew open.

"Whoa!" she exclaimed.

Alice stepped into a black abyss. She caught herself from falling by gripping onto the doorknob, one leg feebly perched on the library floor. Her other leg dangled in emptiness.

Outside the library door, she was surrounded by blackness. The library door floated in empty space. A hollow sound of whooshing pressed against her, as if she were inside a seashell she'd hold to her ear at the ocean shore.

Falling may not hurt in a dream, but Alice didn't feel like testing that notion.

She wriggled until she could grab onto the doorframe and heaved herself back in to the library.

Alice slammed the door shut and collapsed to the floor. *Thank you, lucky stars.*

Okay. That door to the hallway was not an option.

She tried the door to the playroom again and peered through. Sure enough, it was a copy of the library, and there was her own backside at the opposite side of the room.

There must be a way out.

She backed up for some running space and then dashed into the next room. She arrived at the library.

What if I jump instead of run?

She ran toward the open playroom door on the other side of the room and jumped through. She landed in the library.

I must catch up with the king.

Alice checked outside the window. The chess pieces were further along the path. If they passed beyond that grassy hill in the distance, Alice would never catch up to them. She scratched her head.

Maybe there's a limit to the number of libraries.

She ran through the library, into an identical library, and kept on running. Alice puffed onward. She passed through library after library, all of them the same. She passed the same floor-to-ceiling bookshelves, the same wide window that overlooked the back rose garden, the same brick fireplace, the same boring landscape ocean paintings.

After what felt like forever, but was probably only five minutes, she stopped and planted her hands on her knees, puffing to catch her breath. The chess pieces better not have gone over the grassy hill already. A glance out the window got her heart thumping. They were a motor-car's length away from the hill.

There has to be a way out f here.

Alice checked the window. A two-story drop to the rose bushes below. Too dangerous.

Alice gasped, inhaling an epiphany.

If this world is backwards, then maybe all I have to do is walk backwards to get out of the room.

Alice stepped backwards through the door that should have led to the playroom. The room's surroundings opened up to traces of colorful walls and the toys she had once played with when she was a girl. The setting appeared rather reminiscent of the playroom. It was hard to tell because everything looked blurry. But it was working.

Once she was completely inside the next room, she twirled around to scan the place.

Back in the library.

Arrgh!

Alice stomped her foot in frustration, then pulled her shoulders back. Drastic times called for drastic measures. She maneuvered a chair from one painting to another, taking each painting down off its hook and setting it on the floor. She leaned the paintings against the wall.

This was just a dream, she reminded herself.

Her next move was more radical.

She tore the canvas paintings out of their frames, twisted them, and knotted them together into a kind of rope.

She dragged the chair to the window and closed her eyes. "Sorry about the glass, Father," she whispered.

She heaved up the heavy wood chair and smashed it into the window. She turned her face away and clenched her eyes shut against the flying glass.

A gush of smoky cold air rushed in from outside, the opposite of the fresh air she expected to smell. Why did it smell smoky, as if someone set a campfire nearby?

Perhaps that was the mirror-world smell.

She shoved another chair to the broken window and tied her new rope to the chair leg. She tugged on the rope, testing her weight. Knocking out broken glass at the bottom edge of the window frame, she carefully climbed over the ledge. She eased herself down the rope. In the distance, the chess pieces were climbing the hill. She could make it. She could drop to the ground and reach them just in time. Alice dangled above the outdoor lawn, then let herself fall the remaining arm's length.

And fell onto the library floor.

"Oh, come on!" She frowned and wiped her hands against her lemon yellow dress.

The library looked undisturbed, same as always. Even the paintings were back on the walls. The captain in his painting grinned at her.

She stuck her tongue out at him, feeling childish. She didn't care.

Rushing to the unharmed window pane, Alice saw the chess pieces climbing up the grassy hill.

She spun around, looking for a new way out and gasped. Even though all the paintings were still on the wall, a rope of canvases also hung from the ceiling. She squinted. At the top of the rope above the chandelier, there seemed to be a hole where the rope hung from. Weird.

Alice grabbed onto the rope and hand over hand climbed up. Halfway up, she saw out the window that a bishop had fallen over and rolled down the hill. The pawns were rushing down the hill to help the bishop back up. That should win her some time. Alice climbed and pushed against the chandelier for leverage to get herself up through the hole in the ceiling.

She ended up in the cold fire of the library's fireplace.

Alice screamed, and stomped her foot in the cold embers.

"There has to be a way out," she said to the annoying library.

She gazed up the chimney. *Aha!* A light shone from above. The sides were coated in powder, no doubt the soot from the many fires before.

She rubbed the soot between her fingers. This powder couldn't have been soot. It was white and felt like soap.

"Soap powder?"

She grimaced at the filmy-like soap covering, but pressed herself against the brick walls upward through the chimney.

She paused halfway through and braced herself with her feet on the opposite side of the chimney. Her hands free, she spat into her hands and rubbed the white powder into her palms.

Alice inhaled. The grains dissolved into a lotion that smelled like peaches. *Yum!* She rubbed the lotion over her face and checked her hands. Spotless.

Okay, so maybe this reverse world, this mirror land, wasn't all bad. If only she could escape the library and see if she could track down Jack.

Alice resumed climbing up the soap-covered chimney. At the very top, she pulled herself up and out of a large hole made from dirt. She looked for the chess pieces. They were gone. Alice's disappointment set in at missing the chance to connect with the king and become the queen of their group, but when she examined her surroundings, the disappointment vanished.

She was surrounded by sapphire grass, emerald skies, and flowers exhibiting the colors of all the other jewels. Alice bubbled at the excitement of exploring this land.

She'd just climbed out of a rabbit hole into a bright world. Finally. She smiled and sighed and yawned.

Why did she want to take a nap?

Was it that in this mirror world everything was opposite, so only people who were excited would fall asleep and those who were exhausted had insomnia?

She didn't care.

"I must not fall asleep. If I do, I might wake up in the real world and that must not happen. Not yet. I need to find those chess pieces. I need to find some cake or mushroom to make me small. Once I'm small enough, I can be their queen. Once I'm queen, I will know what it is to be an eight-horse woman. Once I'm that eight-horse woman, I will be able to speak to Jack with confidence and charisma. I will know what to say to him, and he will love me the same way he did when we first became lovers. I must not fall asleep."

Alice fell asleep.

8. Jack and Troy

Your lips are a red, red rose.
I wish to pluck them.

ALICE felt soft caresses and gentle kisses on her hips and inner thighs. Voices whispered.

"Her skin is so smooth," one male's rumbling voice said with admiration. She recognized this voice, but from where?

A finger glided along her thigh. Alice tingled.

"Yes," the other male voice said, also familiar somehow. "I wonder if her petals are full of morning dew."

She opened her eyes and gasped. Two giants towered above her: Jack, her boyfriend, and Troy, her neighbor. Her raised skirt exposed her naked hips, her panties nowhere to be seen. Troy had a finger between her legs.

"Hey!" Alice tried to push her skirt down. How did Jack and Troy get to be so big? And why was Troy touching her this way? Why was Jack letting him? She managed to push Troy's finger away.

Oh yeah. I'm dreaming. I suppose that explains my panties disappearing.

A quick glance around revealed she was no bigger than the daisies that surrounded her. So Jack and Troy didn't grow into giants, Alice had simply shrunk down to the size of a chess piece. That's what she wanted, wasn't it? But now here were Jack and Troy, ridiculously huge.

Oh, well. I could practice talking to Jack as if I'm a queen.

Alice sat up. She closed her eyes, took in a deep breath of courage, and opened her eyes.

"Jack," Alice called out. "I want us to be the way we were. That's what I meant when I asked you to treat me like a queen. Both of us deserve each other's devoted love, and I know we can do that. I know because we behaved that way in the beginning of our relationship. At least, that's the way *you* treated me."

Her voice died down on that last remark, but she felt pretty good at how she expressed herself. She sounded confident enough that if she spoke the same way when she woke up, perhaps Jack would desire her again. So why did Jack have a blank expression on his face?

"What a strange flower this is." Troy brushed his gigantic fingertip across the fabric over Alice's breasts. "Look how lovely these firm things are, Jack. Is this where the pollen's nectar comes from?"

Alice's pushed Troy's stimulating touch away.

"No," Jack chuckled. "You're not even close. This is an *Alisian Cartesian*, pretty common around these parts. Nothing special. This flower tends to wander all over the map."

Alice's stomach fell. Jack hadn't heard her. In fact, he seemed to think she wasn't even human.

Two nearby flowers laughed. At least, they looked like flowers, but maybe they were Lois and Carol, her sister and her sister's girlfriend. Alice sat up to get a better look. One of the naked daisies had a smile that resembled Lois. The other had eyes like Carol's.

"She's common, all right," the one that looked like Lois sneered. "Her Latin name is *Cheapus Trampus*."

The Carol flower howled with laughter. "Yeah, of the *Commonus Slutus* variety."

Alice stood and clenched her fists. "Hey!"

"So where is her nectar, Jack?" Troy ignored her outburst and didn't glance at the Lois and Carol flowers mocking her.

Jack nudged Alice back to the ground. "Right here." He tucked his pinky, the girth of her ankles, right up her dress and stroked the inner folds of her pussy.

Alice sucked in a breath at the surprise move, so delicious. She studied Jack's face, admiring his cute look of concentration while trying to map her, and feeling a zing every time he had a brush with success.

"Let me see," Troy said.

Troy's pinky soon replaced Jack's. Alice stiffened, willing her hands to push Troy away, but knowing this was a dream, desire won her over. He stimulated her sweet spot, summoning her moisture, making her drip.

"Come on," Lois said to Carol. "Let's show them what pretty flowers really look like."

They kissed each other, their arms and legs entwining. Yellow petals fell from their lips.

Troy's finger strolled up to Alice's clit. With the pad of his finger, he circled her wearing an expression of fascination. Alice squeezed her thighs around him, and clamped her hands on her breasts to appease her aching nipples.

"This is a magnificent bud, Jack," he said. "It should bloom quite nicely. I think it just needs some stimulation. Come feel it."

Jack shrugged. He placed an obligatory fingertip where Troy's had been. As Jack stared up at the sky with a thoughtful pose, he flicked across Alice's clit expertly.

Alice sighed, delighting in his touch.

"It has potential." Jack removed his finger. "But it's not my cup of tea. I much prefer those flowers over there." He nodded to Lois and Carol whose bodies writhed against each other.

Alice sat up. Jack stroked the bare backs and backsides of Lois and Carol as they squirmed, locked in their embrace.

Lois pulled back from Carol and snickered at Alice. "You do realize he thinks of us when he closes his eyes, don't you? That's why he closes his eyes when he's in bed with you. You are nothing to him."

Alice clenched the fabric of her dress at her heart.

Troy stroked Alice's hair. "Don't you worry, there, pretty flower. There's a place for you in everyone's heart."

Alice studied the ring on her pinky. What had her reflection said?

Let the ring guide you.

The ring wasn't vibrating or making any indication that this was her path. What did its silence mean?

Perhaps these fears of him desiring another woman were the feelings she had to let go of.

Alice rose to her feet and ran. She had to get away from this garden. She had to find those chess pieces and become their queen. She had to be that eight-horse woman. She had to get Jack back.

9. The White Queen

*The people you need in your life
Are the ones you already know.*

ALICE skittered from the garden and followed a path of round, scarlet stones toward a distant clearing surrounded by trees. A chess piece claimed the center and was smoothing out her dress. Unfortunately, it was the white queen. The role of white queen was already taken? Could there be more than two queens? What about the black queen? Was there already a black queen or was there a vacancy Alice could fill for that position?

Alice bit her lip. Maybe the white queen could be a mentor and at least show her how to have the confidence, grace, and charisma she needed.

She neared the white queen who stood only a bit taller than herself. "Your Majesty!"

The queen didn't look up. She continued smoothing out her dress.

Alice ran closer… and ended up inside the library.

She shook her fists at the room. "Oh, for crying out loud!"

Alice paced back and forth. This had to have been the most frustrating dream she had ever had. At least she was normal size again.

She needed to relax. There had to be a way out without falling back in the library all the time.

Alice puffed out a deep breath.

If this is a world of opposites, then maybe trying for the opposite of what I desire will get what I want. I want to see the queen, so instead I'll hide from the queen and maybe she'll appear.

Alice ducked under the table. The queen didn't appear.

She waited a few heartbeats. When no one entered the room, Alice said aloud, "I don't wish to see the queen. I don't wish to see the queen."

Alas, this dream obeyed her wish and no queen appeared.

Arrgh! Alice beat the floor with her fists.

The carpet had a slight rip beside her fists. Alice tugged at the rip. The carpet tore like paper, revealing a latch to a trap door. This had to be a way out.

Alice tugged on the latch. The trap door came up. She smiled and squinted at a bright light. The strong scent of sweet butterscotch wafted up.

She pushed the trap door open and followed its wide wooden ladder down into its sweet-smelling brightness. Lovely.

At the bottom of the ladder, she spun and came face to face with a wall of chartreuse grass, vertical as any wall. She'd never seen a wall of grass before.

She blinked, not sure what to make of it.

Suddenly, she was yanked right into the grassy wall, as if she were a magnet to metal. Her chest hit the grass hard.

"Oof."

A woman's voice commanded, "Get up, young lady."

Alice's head spun.

She squinted at the bright, white light, getting her bearings. A magnetic pull hadn't been responsible for her planting her on the wall of grass. It was gravity. Her brain finally caught up with her sight. She was lying on the ground.

"Get up this instant," the woman barked again.

Alice quickly got to her feet and gasped. It was the white queen chess piece with a ghostly white face, white hair twisted into a high up-do, and an elegant, lacy white gown.

Alice recovered her manners and curtsied. "Your Majesty."

"Arise, maiden." The queen gestured elegantly. Her voice sounded familiar.

Alice blinked, scrutinizing the white face. By imagining the queen with Caribbean-colored eyes, crimson lips, and ginger hair, the queen could have look exactly like her sister's girlfriend Carol.

Alice gulped. So strange that the queen resembled Carol.

"You look a travesty." The queen yanked Alice closer by her arm and patted down Alice's yellow dress. Queen Carol slapped Alice's dress at her shins, her thighs, her behind, her shoulders. Puffs of dirt flew off.

Alice held back a sneeze that threatened to embarrass her more in front of the queen.

"What a disgrace." The queen adjusted Alice's dress, shifting the waist to properly rest on her hips, tugging at the scoop neckline to properly rest on her breasts, untying and tying the lace behind her neck. This Carol doppelganger smelled like butterscotch.

Alice liked the smell, and there was something comforting about being handled so roughly.

"Absolutely disgusting." Queen Carol frowned and fiddled with Alice's hair, stroking and teasing the hair as if setting it back to its proper shape.

Alice smiled, despite the harsh words. Funny how Alice felt adored even though Carol kept saying what a mess she was.

"That's better." Queen Carol eyed Alice's

forehead and swept up any remaining straggling strands of hair into the top of her head. She frowned at Alice. "Now come with me."

The queen glided above the ground up a grassy hill, different from the one the other chess pieces had marched over.

Alice hustled to catch up with her. "Where are we going?"

The queen rolled her eyes. "You wish to become a queen, don't you?"

Alice's mind raced. All her troubles with Jack could be resolved if she became queen in this dream. "Yes!"

The queen smiled regally, looking down on Alice. "Then that is what we will do. We must start you on your journey *toute suite*."

Alice knew that was French for "right away."

At last, she would become a queen.

10. The Chessboard

Some prefer to be the player,
Some prefer to be the one played.
Which are you?

"THERE." The queen pointed.

Alice followed the queen's arm, which pointed down the hill in front of them to a vast view of acres upon acres of squares. All the squares alternated colors, black and white.

"A chessboard?" Alice asked and punched the palm of her hand with understanding. "Ah, I shall be a pawn in this game, moving from square to square until I reach the other end and become queen." She smiled at the genius of it.

Queen Carol squinted at her, assessing. "Are you

sure you wish to take on this adventure, Alice?"

"Of course!" Alice smiled her best, most endearing smile. "If I become queen, I'll gain the confidence and charisma I need to win back Jack. I'll be an eight-horse woman."

The queen scowled. "A eight-horse woman?"

"Long story. You were saying?"

The queen eyed her up and down. "You don't *look* as heavy as an eight-horse woman. Two or three horses, maybe, but eight?"

Alice huffed, "You think I weigh as much as three horses?"

"Small ones," the queen said to calm her. It didn't work.

Alice spoke through gritted teeth. "You were saying?"

"Every adventure comes with a lesson." She peered at Alice, as if examining her soul. Queen Carol finally said, "Let me warn you of what you will face."

Alice nodded eagerly. She was ready for this.

The queen continued. "You must traverse six squares starting from Square Two and ending at Square Eight to become a queen. On your journey to Square Three, remember this." She raised a finger to emphasize her point and chanted, " 'Become the steam, become the coal, become the track to find your soul. Become the wheels to run your test. You'll find the one who'll help you best.' "

Alice's stomach fluttered with nerves. "What do

you mean?"

"Please, Alice. Don't interrupt. Soon you'll arrive at Square Three." She recited, " 'Bugs and critters are to be greeted to show how you deserve to be treated.' "

Alice shivered. *Greet bugs?* Maybe she could escape the first square quickly if it was to be full of bugs. She gulped and nodded.

"On your way to Square Four," the queen said picking up her sing-song voice. " 'Forget yourself and shame yourself, decide to cherish or despise yourself.' "

Alice nodded, even though she didn't understand. She said the words in her head to remember them.

"At Square Four, here is what you'll find: 'Two brothers, your lover, opposing each other. You wish to know one, but don't know the other.' "

Alice tingled. *Two brothers? As lovers? That could be fun.*

"On your way to Square Five, 'you drip with excitement, you're wet with desire, but not everything wet will come from a fire.' "

Alice shivered, this time with anticipation. She had no clue what the queen was talking about, but that trip to the third square sounded pretty darn delicious.

"At Square Five, take heed: 'To be a queen you must understand, every queen in the land. Spell the word 'but,' not the word 'and,' to unlock the troubles a queen has at hand.' " Queen Carol cleared her throat and peered at Alice, as if willing her to understand the importance of her commands. "You'll then chase your way to Square Six. 'While it's good to wish to grab a he-pole, the queen will show what kind of people blindly follow the path she has taken, a path of royalty much mistaken.' "

A 'he-pole?' Alice snickered at what the queen probably meant by that.

"At Square Six, 'you'll see that the ribs, the blood, and the skin are not enough. A woman's heart must be properly packaged.' As you move to the seventh square—"

Alice held up her hand. "Wait a moment. That last thing you said? 'The ribs, the blood, and the skin are not enough. A woman's heart must be properly packaged.' That didn't rhyme."

The queen stared at Alice, a blank expression on her face. "What's a 'rhyme'?"

Alice shook her head. "Never mind. Please continue."

The queen waited. "Please continue…"

Alice rolled her eyes. She curtsied. "Please continue, Your Majesty."

"Very well. As you move to Square Seven, 'you'll learn how a horse and a lion will just never heed how the best resolution is what they both need.' When you arrive at Square Seven…" Queen Carol lowered her eyes and sighed.

Alice leaned in. "What's wrong?"

"It's about the seventh square." The queen shook her head, unhappy, and was that fear on her face?

"What is it?" She got a sinking feeling in her gut. Was this journey to become queen a good idea? "What happens at the seventh square?"

The queen took a deep breath. " 'I fear you'll not know the answer to this one. When the black knight forces you into decision, the sad truth of it all is, to follow your lie, you must let the secret of your little deaths die.' "

"I'll be meeting a black knight?"

Queen Carol bit her lip and nodded, sadness in her big eyes. "When you do come across the black knight, watch what the knight says. The black knight may wake you up."

That would be bad. Alice must not wake up before the coronation. She had to become a queen in this dream before confronting Jack. She had to understand the secrets on being confident and charismatic. Perhaps if Alice just focused on avoiding any black knight on her travels, all would be okay.

"As for Jack," Queen Carol said, "he, too, has the power to wake you up."

Alice frowned. "Should I avoid him, then?"

"On the contrary. He will help you on your journey. Just be careful not to aggravate him or cause him any stress. As long as he's happy, you'll find your true calling."

Alice nodded, balancing in her head all the tips on how she must behave on her adventure. She would need to be careful, and consider whom she journeyed with every step of the way.

"So." The queen clapped her hands once, waking Alice from her thoughts. "Next is the journey to the final square. Your trip to the eighth square will help you. 'You want to unlock the why of your lover. The reason he loves you, you wish to discover. On this piercing journey to your coronation, you'll learn of the answer before the destination.' "

Alice sighed with relief. Yes, she did indeed want to know why Jack loved her. Perhaps knowing that would help her know what she could do to keep him.

Alice asked, "And when I arrive at the final square?"

"At last you will have your coronation." The queen nodded. "You will become queen and will be given a final riddle at the climax of your journey. But I've said too much." She peered down the hill. "You'll need to get to your starting position. You see that square in the second row?"

The queen pointed to the square in front of the queen's placement in the beginning of a chess game.

Alice nodded. She knew the game. "You want me to go to queen two?"

"Precisely."

Giddiness bubbled up in her chest. How exciting to play a pawn in live chess. "Last one there is a rotten egg!" She laughed and ran toward the square.

But an odd thing—the chessboard stretched further and further away from her.

"Hey!" she yelled, breathlessly, pumping her legs as fast as she could to run down the grassy slope.

The queen stood beside her and chuckled regally. "Tsk, tsk. You'll never get there that way."

Alice checked her feet on the ground. The grassy earth beneath her moved as if she were running, but just the spot she ran on moved. The rest of the ground stayed fixed in place.

What was going on?

Alice stopped and caught her breath.

"What am I doing wrong?" Alice's managed to say gulping down air.

With a raised chin, the queen peered down at Alice. "You're not letting yourself go."

"I'm not?"

"Yes."

"I am?"

"No." Queen Carol scowled.

"But you said 'Yes.' "

The queen huffed. "I meant, yes, you're not. Letting yourself go."

Alice scratched her head. What was the queen who looked so much like her sister's friend Carol trying to say?

The queen shook her head and waved her hand, as if batting away a fly. "The point is that there is only one way to meet those waiting for you at your starting square. You must get them to *want* to meet you."

"How do I do that?" Alice glanced up at the queen.

The queen took Alice's hands, more gently than Alice would have expected, and crossed Alice's arms over her torso.

"Start by embracing yourself," the queen said. "The more you appreciate yourself, the more others will appreciate you."

Okay, that she could do. She wanted to play the game. Alice closed her eyes and squeezed herself. She heard the queen move behind her.

Queen Carol embraced Alice from behind, her arms wrapped around Alice's waist. She whispered sadly into Alice's ear. "Always remember who you are."

11. The Train

Become the steam, become the coal,
Become the track to find your soul,
Become the wheels to run your test.
You'll find the one who'll help you best.

Square Two

As ALICE embraced herself with eyes closed, Queen Carol behind seemed to vibrate. The queen's entire body shook. Was she having a seizure?

Alice opened her eyes. Lord! She was sitting in a moving, clicking-clacking train. The queen was nowhere to be seen. Sitting across from Alice in the coach, however, perched a stunning woman.

The woman didn't seem to notice Alice. She just

adjusted her kiss-me red wide brim hat and smoothed down the knee-high hem of her take-me red dress. She then gazed at the passing greenery, which, Alice supposed, should have been called *bluery* instead of greenery, because the trees were blue.

The coach door slid open. In stepped Jack. Alice's heartbeat quickened. It was good to see Jack in her dream. Now she could play with him and see what she could do to rekindle their love. Alice remembered Queen Carol's warning, though. She must be careful not to agitate Jack in any way, or else she'll wake up.

Jack hitched up his trousers and sang to no one in particular, "I'm just a man looking for love, wanting a woman to be my dove. Though I fear I may not find a trace, I feel in my heart I've come to the right place."

The radiant woman across from Alice gazed upon Jack and smiled at his song.

"Jack," Alice beamed. "I'm here." She waved to catch his eye.

But Jack, standing in the aisle, closed his eyes and kept on singing. "I've searched the world, and heaven and hell. I know my love is here, I can tell. She blossoms like spring, with petals to pluck. Once in my arms, I'll give her a—"

"Jack!" Alice laughed. "I'm here."

Jack scratched his head, but didn't look at her, and said, "How does it go? Ah yes." He took a deep breath and resumed his singing, "Once in my arms, I'll give her a kiss of luck." He turned to the gorgeous woman sitting across from Alice and said to her, "And there my love sits, my lifelong goal. I give you my body, my heart and my soul."

Alice sat stunned. "What? Jack!"

But he didn't turn to her.

Did he not see her? She was there, wasn't she?

She examined her hands, but couldn't see them. Nothing was there. In fact, none of her body was there. She was invisible to herself. By the way Jack didn't respond to her, her voice probably didn't make any sound either.

She heaved a sigh. Tears threatened, but she gulped them back. What good would they do?

The train rumbled toward its destination, wherever that was. Jack knelt and sang, a hand on his heart. He sang on and his voice carried over the clicking and clacking of the train. In fact, the chug-chug of the train accompanied his song, like an orchestral percussion ensemble.

The woman blushed at Jack's attentions and put her hands on her reddening cheeks.

I want that. I want to be seen that way. Alice sighed and wiped furiously at the wetness on her cheeks.

The coach door slid open. Four more men, dressed as barber shop quartet singers, strode into the coach and crowded the woman, beside Jack. Maybe they could help her get Jack to see her.

Alice stood and tapped on their shoulders. "Hello? Can you help me?"

They didn't respond.

"You can't see me, either?"

With no indication of noticing Alice's presence, the four men picked up the harmony beautifully, highlighting Jack's growling bass voice.

Alice clenched her fist, but couldn't leave. The music was so beautiful. But it wasn't for her. Unbelievable. All that attention to another woman from Jack.

Could this ride get any worse?

The door rattled opened for a third time. More men strode in. The train's ticket taker, the conductor, and it seemed about twenty more men tumbled into the coach. They added their voices and the quintet became a full-fledged choir, adding their basses and tenors to the mix.

Alice grunted in frustration. She sat down and had to press herself against her seat as the incoming men squeezed against her. Though they didn't see her, she could feel their warm bodies and musky scents press against her.

Alice wanted to leave, but the door was blocked. Why couldn't she get such amazing attention? Why couldn't she get *any* attention?

Then an idea came to her and her breath quickened. Alice maneuvered through the crowd, crawling under legs, squeezing between men's chests, her nipples hardening at the contact.

She steered herself onto the woman's lap. The

woman squirmed a bit, but didn't push Alice off. Alice was invisible to her, too. Good.

Now all gazes and voices were directed toward Alice. At least, that was how it felt. Perhaps they were singing to the lady, but Alice shoved that out of mind.

She took in a deep breath, smiled, and let their attention sink in.

This attention was what she wanted after all, wasn't it?

What was Queen Carol's first riddle?

> *Become the steam, become the coal,*
> *Become the track to find your soul,*
> *Become the wheels to run your test.*
> *You'll find the one who'll help you best.*

Jack gazed at her, singing and caressed her hair. At least it felt like hers and not the pretty lady upon whom she was seated. His voice was steam, was love. She breathed it in deeply.

He wasn't reaching for the woman's hair, Alice told herself. He was reaching for her own.

His warm palm caressed and comforted her. His palm lingered on her neck, then ever downward to rest on Alice's breast. He cupped it and she arched her back to fill Jack's hand, her nipple pebbling and aching for more.

Jack continued singing and tore off his turquoise shirt. The rest of the men stripped off their own shirts, singing all the way.

Alice chuckled at the impromptu display. All those bare chests, all muscular and strong. Her giggles subsided and left behind a prominent ache kindling at her core. Alice wanted to cup her mound and squirm at the sight of the topless men singing her a love song, but she didn't want to get caught.

Wait a second. I'm invisible. I can touch myself as much as I want.

A fire of desire rushed across her skin. She licked her lip. Her core burned like an oven of hot coals. The answer to the queen's riddle seeped inside of Alice. She opened her legs, ready for more clarity.

Jack unbuttoned his pants and unzipped his fly, showing her just how much he wanted her.

Alice bit her lip and scooted forward along the woman's legs, like riding the rails of a train track, to ready herself for Jack.

Jack gazed on Alice's face as she helped guide him into her. He sang softly now right to her. The rest of the choir whispered their accompaniment, along with the chug-chug of the train.

He slipped inside of Alice easily, her wet passion welcoming his gentle thrusts.

Become the steam.

Jack pushed in. Alice moaned.

Become the coal.

Out and in, Alice flushed hot. She understood.

Become the train.

Alice must become the train.

Jack pistoned out and in. The train shook and vibrated, convulsed and shuddered.

Alice pulled Jack's head to her chest and let the engine of her pleasure steer from her pussy, through her pounding heart, to her hardened nipples. She grabbed a fist of Jack's hair and curled her toes, the heat rising.

After her climax, Alice stilled, catching her breath. The world around came back into view: the men singing, the woman, the train.

The singers still sang in her direction, but was this really about herself?

Alice looked behind her to see the woman whose lap she occupied. The woman's face glowed. She looked as much in ecstasy as Alice felt.

She blew out a breath of frustration. The attention was all for the woman. Not for herself.

Alice couldn't understand. What was the answer to Queen Carol's riddle?

I'm just a pawn. I want to be seen. Who can help me best with being seen?

How could anyone help her be seen if no one could see her?

And then Alice understood the queen's riddle. She wasn't supposed to become the train. She needed to become the trainer.

Become the steam, become the coal,
Become the track to find your soul,
Become the wheels to run your test.
You'll find the one who'll help you best.

The answer to the riddle? Train yourself.

Being seen started with Alice. She had to let go of relying on others to validate her worth. She even had to let go of relying on Jack for how she felt about herself. She needed to let herself leave that ball and chain of dependence.

Alice breathed in, then out. Jack kissed her lips, probably thinking he was kissing the woman's lips.

Alice closed her eyes and let herself go.

12. The Blind Man

*Bugs and critters are to be greeted
To show how you deserve to be treated.*

<u>Square Three</u>

A HIGH-PITCHED voice whispered in Alice's ear. "You're a chore. You will always be a chore."

What? Alice opened her eyes. She was leaning against a tree and took a deep breath, orienting herself. Minty air cooled her lungs.

"You're ugly," another tiny voice continued. "You will always be ugly."

Alice batted at her ear.

The voices persisted. "You will always be lonely," and "You will always be lost," and "You will always be unwanted."

"Enough!" Alice pushed off from the tree and swiveled, searching for the origin of the voices. "I don't need such voices constantly around me like flies."

"Not flies," a different and deep voice said. "Bees."

A distinguished gentleman in a pin-striped suit stepped out from behind a tree. He stared with vacant, milky eyes, an ebony cane waving in front of him. He was blind. The man reminded Alice of one of her young university professors she'd greatly admired for his chiseled face and wise words.

"Who are you?" Alice asked, curious, not afraid.

"I am the Heart Whisperer. I'm here to help you with those voices. Those bees."

Alice checked around. "I don't see any bees."

"Not 'bees.' *Bees.*"

What did he mean? Alice waited for him to clarify.

He spelled out, "B – E – apostrophe – S. Be's."

"Oh. *Be's,*" Alice parroted. That still made about as much sense as acupuncture for porcupines, but he seemed wise enough, so she waited for an explanation. Professors always like to explain things to anyone around.

In the next moment, a large orange cat with white stripes jumped into the blind man's free arm, balancing easily.

"Oh, ho!" The blind man laughed. "It's my favorite time traveler."

Alice's heart swelled with joy. "My dear Cheshire cat!"

The blind man dropped his cane to pet the cat. "You know him?"

"I certainly do." Alice approached the professor to pet the cat.

The cat raised his head to meet Alice's ready palm. His purr increased in intensity.

"I met the rascal on my previous trip to this wonderland." Alice put her face close to the sweet cat's whiskers. "Did you come from my future?"

The cat pushed his head against Alice's cheek. "I have seen it."

"How does my future look?"

"Terribly grim. Not good at all. It just goes from wonderful to horrible, and all in one day."

Alice jerked away. "How dreadful!"

The cat shrugged its shoulders. "Perhaps it will be the opposite for you since you experience your timeline in the opposite direction as me. I always get the order of things mixed up."

"I hope that's the case." Alice wiped the cat's shedding fur off her hands on her dress. "You'll soon be seeing me on a train, then in a garden, and then in the library. When you see Jack, tell him I'm fine."

"Weren't you there?"

"Well, yes."

"Then you can tell him yourself." He grinned that disconcerting mouthful of teeth.

Alice tried to work out what the cat meant, but got distracted by how he faded out and disappeared in a blink.

The blind man chuckled. "Clever cat, that one."

"Indeed." Alice scowled and twirled a lock of her hair. Confusing, this backwards time-travel stuff.

The tiny voices came back, whispering annoyingly in her ears.

"You will always be alone."

"You will always be unloved."

"You will always be ignored."

Alice swatted them away.

The blind man cleared his throat. "Now about your 'be' problem. I can train those voices to speak much sweeter to you."

"You can?" Alice swatted at the invisible sounds. "How?"

"Why, with honey of course." The gentleman with milky eyes stepped to within a breath of her. "No voices are sweeter than those from honey be's."

Alice smiled. His breath reminded her of childhood breakfast honey. She inhaled and closed her eyes to enjoy his scent. He brushed his hands up her arms, placed his hands on her shoulders, and gently guided her to face away from him.

She opened her eyes.

He traced his fingertips along her shoulders to the tied lace of her dress behind her neck. "May I remove your dress?"

Was this a necessary part of her journey? What had the queen said?

Bugs and critters are to be greeted,
To show how you deserve to be treated.

Alice nodded. She wasn't supposed to get rid of the voices that bugged her. She had to retrain them. That's what this Heart Whisperer could do for her. Besides, the man was blind. It wasn't as if he'd see anything.

"Yes," Alice said.

The lace loosened at her neck. He guided the stretchy waistline past her waist. Her dress pooled at her feet.

The man drew his fingers across her naked shoulders and fiddled her bra straps. "And this?"

She reached behind, unclipped the cotton bra, and let it slide off her arms and drop to the ground.

He whispered, "Are you wearing anything else?"

Alice stepped out of her shoes to be barefoot. "No."

She'd been panty-free ever since she awoke as a flower in the garden.

"Then let's get started, shall we?"

She took in a deep breath and exhaled. "Yes."

"As you may have noticed from the scent of my breath, my saliva is made of honey. I can help the voices be drawn to your sweetness, but you too must absorb the honey and make it be a part of you."

Alice curled her toes with anticipation, feeling the

cold earth at her feet. "What do I need to do?"

"Let me kiss your body and coat you with honey. I will say certain phrases and you must repeat them. Do you understand?"

Alice's nipples hardened. This wasn't cheating on Jack. It was just a dream.

She figured out the answer to the queen's riddle. Treat yourself sweetly.

This Heart Whisperer was the key to unlock that door. He was a necessary part of her journey.

"I understand," she said.

"May I begin?"

Alice shook her body loose and closed her eyes. "Yes."

The first kiss at her shoulder dripped warm and thick, her skin sensing a droplet crawling down to her breast. A second kiss to the same shoulder. Then a third.

Alice kept her eyes closed and resisted the temptation to brush away the tickle of drops, some sliding down to her breast, others down her back.

He whispered, "You will be respected."

He kissed the crook of her neck. She had to tilt her head to let him reach. Goosebumps rippled along her arms and legs.

"Say it," he said. "You will be respected."

Alice nodded. "I will be respected."

The honey on her shoulder cooled in the minty fresh air, tightening fast and sticky against her skin.

He pressed his lips to her other shoulder, honey spilling from his kisses. The voices around her would soon no longer be hurtful. A sadness clumped inside her gut. Over the years, Alice had become used to those hurtful voices. Their familiarity had in some twisted way kept her company. Soon they would be gone, that family of hurtful voices. Droplets of the honey cried down her chest, mourning the end of those voices.

"You will be admired," the blind man said.

Alice swallowed. "I will be admired."

He kissed her arms. Alice opened her eyes watching this man assist her on her journey to being treated like a queen. He sauntered to the front of her—tall, distinguished—this man who was not Jack.

A trickle of doubt arrived. Wasn't she supposed to train herself?

He kissed the palms of her hands. It tickled. The honey on her arms shined wet and sweetened the scent of the minty air.

Yes, I do need to train myself, but that means knowing what or who I need to recruit to help me.

She smiled at that realization.

"You will be loved," the blind man said.

Alice looked up at him and repeated his words, "I will be loved," her heart aching. She could not tell if she was lying to herself.

The Heart Whisperer stepped closer to her and embraced her, massaging the drops of honey on her back into her skin.

"You will be treasured," he said.

Alice needed to take a deep breath for that one. She repeated the words. "I will be treasured."

His hands reached down to her rear. She released some nervous laughter.

"Relax." His hands felt hot on her behind.

Alice breathed deeply.

He clenched her plumpy flesh with sticky fists. "You will be desired."

Another breath and Alice repeated his words, "I will be desired."

He stepped behind her and kissed her shoulders again. More droplets dripped like syrup down to her breasts. He held her from behind, caressing her breasts and molding them, coating them with his honey.

Sweet sparks popped across her skin.

He squeezed her, holding her against his chest. "You will be craved."

Through unsteady breaths, Alice puffed out the words, ready to believe them. "I will be craved."

He spun her around and planted a fierce kiss on her mouth. She closed her eyes, accepting the sudden pass at her. Honey spilled onto her tongue. The sweetest she'd ever tasted.

He broke the kiss, a firm grip on her arms. She opened her eyes and gasped. The milky color of his eyes was gone. The blind man was no longer blind.

"You will be seen." He directed a stern gaze right at her, as if he stared at her soul. His amber eyes seemed to change shades, like whirling spots of honey, from dark to light amber and back again. "Say it."

Alice blinked aware of her surroundings, aware of being naked, aware of being covered with sticky honey, aware of his sweet taste mixing with the cool minty air at her lips.

He shook her. "Say it."

Alice swallowed the honey. "I will be seen."

Tiny voices chanted at her ears. "You will be seen. You will be seen, Alice. You will always be seen."

Alice shivered at the lesson. Not only must she train herself, but she must also treat herself sweetly.

13. The Forgotten Forest

Forget yourself and shame yourself,
Decide to cherish or despise yourself.

To Square Four

ALICE didn't feel like she was covered in honey. She felt unnaturally normal.

My skin should feel sticky, shouldn't it?

She patted her shoulders, down her torso and legs. She couldn't feel or see any honey anywhere on her body.

She turned to ask the blind man why and sucked in a breath. *That's right. He's no longer blind.* He was staring at her, scanning her face and naked body.

Alice covered her breasts and backed away from

him. Her cheeks flamed hot.

He leaned against a tree, his amber eyes swirling their different shades, all of them shades of kindness. "Is there something the matter?"

Alice picked up her bra and turned her back to him. "No, it's just," she fastened the clasp of the bra behind her back. "You're staring at me." Where were her panties? Oh, that's right. They were left behind in the garden.

"Shall I avert my eyes?"

Alice took a deep breath, her heart fluttering in her chest, and turned around. "No. I think I like being seen this way."

The Heart Whisperer smiled. "You will always be seen, Alice."

His gaze drifted down to her breasts, her hips, her legs, and up again, slowly, languidly.

Alice's pulse quickened. She picked up her dress and slipped it over, acting as if he wasn't there. She smiled under the fabric, glad he was there. Adjusting the waistline on her hips, she had a troubled thought.

I've wasted so many years of my life thinking horrible things about myself. If only I had known long ago that I can be desirable and craved, I could have become a much better person.

After tying the lace behind her neck, she glanced at the Heart Whisperer.

His eyes seemed to be welling up with tears.

"What's wrong?" she asked.

"You will soon forget your name." He released a sad sigh.

Alice must have heard him wrong. How could someone forget their own name? Did he think she'd fall, hit her head, and get amnesia?

"I know, it sounds odd, but you have yet to cross the Forgotten Forest, the place where everyone forgets who they are." He shook his head, frowning.

Anything could happen in this wonderland. Still, avoiding the woods should be easy enough. "Where is this Forgotten Forest?"

"I forget."

Okay, not as easy as I had hoped.

The Heart Whisperer pushed off from the tree and stepped closer. "It's true that you appreciate yourself more, but you don't yet know who you are, so in those woods you will quickly forget your name." He gazed off into the distance and fell silent for some moments. Then he smiled at her sadly. "Ah, well, it can be good to forget your name in some situations."

Alice cocked her head. "How so?"

He shrugged. "If you're in a dark hallway with a boa constrictor around your torso, and the snake is squeezing the life out of you, and you knock on your parents' bedroom door, they'll ask who it is, you won't reply because you won't remember your name, and they'll rush to the door thinking something is wrong, they'll see the snake, and your father will take a carving knife and kill the snake while being careful not to spill any blood on the carpet, and you'll be saved. That's a situation where not knowing your name could come in handy."

Alice scowled. "I suppose, but—"

He raised a hand up to stop her from finishing. "Listen. For now, the most important thing is to remember your name. Never forget who you are."

Alice stiffened. *Never forget who you are.* Queen Carol had said the same thing. Was it a warning?

The Heart Whisperer pointed to a path. "It's time for you to go. Your next adventure awaits you."

Alice thanked the kind man with the honey kisses and the amber eyes and followed the path ahead.

As she ambled down the grassy footpath, she heard him say, "Poor, lost Alice."

I must remember my name. Alice. Alice. Alice.

The Heart Whisperer's voice was fading. "Lost Alice. Lost Alice." His chant coaxed her into wanting to repeat him.

I must remember my name. Alice. Lost Alice. Lost Alice.

The path led into a crowd of trees. Could this be the Forgotten Forest?

Alice's head spun. She couldn't let the fuzziness cloud her memory.

She recited aloud, "Lost Alice, lost Alice, lost Alice." She let her tongue memorize the way the words formed in her mouth. "Lost Alice, lost Alice, lost Alice."

She pushed a sapphire tree branch out of her way, but it snapped back in her face and struck her cheek.

"Ow!" She rubbed the sting and let her tongue make the syllables it remembered. "Lost-al-iss-lost-al-iss-lost. All is lost. All is lost." She frowned. "All is lost? Why do I think all is lost if I still remember my name. It's…" She worked her mind, tumbling around all the possibilities of what her name might be. "Is it Francine? Sarah? Traci?" She shook her head. "No. I don't think it's any of those. I can't remember what my name is. All truly *is* lost. That's why I was saying so before."

She trekked deeper into the woods. Perhaps something in the woods would help her remember who she was, something that could trigger a memory.

A light chocolate-tasting mist hung in the air.

A woman's voice called out, "Hi there!"

Where did the voice come from? She looked around and saw a young woman in a golden dress skipping toward her.

The woman in the golden dress asked, "Who are you?"

"I don't know. I can't even remember my own name. It worries me. I mean, who forgets their own name?"

The woman nodded, eyes wide. "I know. It's happened to me too. I can't remember who I am."

"Hmm. Maybe we should create names for ourselves. Just until we remember what our real names are."

The woman reached out and lightly touched her arm. "Great idea. What should my name be?"

"How do you feel?"

"Like a lucky duck for running into you."

"Hmm. Let's not call you Duck. How about Buck?"

The woman tapped her chin. "Buck. Buck. Buck." She smiled. "I like it. What shall we call you?"

Hmm. She licked her lips to come up with a good name. Her lips tasted sweet. "Call me Honey."

Buck held out her hand. "Nice to meet you, Honey."

Honey shook the woman's hand. Buck's hand was soft and smooth. "A pleasure to meet you, Buck."

The woman didn't let go of Honey's hand. "Do you remember anything before you came into this forest?"

"Just about everything. I have a boyfriend, I went through a mirror." Honey decided it prudent not to mention the rubbing those boys gave her at the garden. "I remember meeting a queen who gave me all sorts of advice for my journey. I met a blind man who warned me of this forest, and now I'm here."

Buck took Honey's hand in both of her own. "Did the queen have any advice on how to get out of this forest?"

"I don't think so."

"Are you sure? What did she say?"

Honey slipped her hands away from Buck's and scratched her head. " 'Forget yourself and shame yourself, decide to cherish or despise yourself.' "

Buck placed her hands on her hips. "That's not very helpful advice, if you ask me."

"I suppose it isn't." Honey smacked her lips. "Strange, how the surrounding mist tastes chocolaty. At least, it *should* be strange, shouldn't it? Or does all forest mist taste chocolaty and did I just forget that fact?"

Buck shrugged. "Come along, Honey. Let's find a way out of these woods."

Honey walked beside Buck in the forest. The leaves crumpled and unraveled like they were breathing. How odd. The rocks on the path they followed resembled tiny crumpets. Even odder. The birds overhead hyperventilated like happy puppies. So very odd.

"You said you have a boyfriend?" Buck's stride matched Honey's own.

"Yes, and I remember his name. His name's Jack. I think he's why I'm here in this wonderland."

"What do you mean?"

Honey bit her lip. Should she really say all that she was going through? Her shoulders relaxed. There was something comforting about talking to a stranger. "I'm here to learn about who I am and how to be treated like a queen." She glanced over at Buck to see how she was taking it.

Buck made an agreeing sound and nodded, so Honey continued.

How to say this? "That is, I want Jack to treat me like a queen."

"So he's not treating you like a queen now?"

Honey nodded. "That's right."

"And you think it has more to do with you than it does with him?"

Honey exhaled a sad sigh and nodded. "Yeah. Probably."

"You can't expect to be cherished until you first cherish yourself, right?" Buck nudged Honey with her shoulder.

"Right." Honey's chest warmed at how Buck understood her feelings. Her friendly camaraderie was warming too.

Honey strolled further beside Buck along the path of crumpets, beside the breathing leaves, and under the panting birds.

"I bet he's so very handsome," Buck said, after some time.

"Who?"

"Your boyfriend Jack."

Honey smiled. "He is. Why do you say so?"

"Because only women of incredible beauty can land a handsome man."

Honey blushed. "I'm not that beautiful."

Buck rushed in front of her and stood in her way.

Honey had to stop.

"Of course you are! You can have any man you desire. Or woman." She winked and touched her shoulder.

Lord, is this woman hitting on me?

Honey brushed past her and continued down the stone path. She laced a lock of her hair behind her ear and spoke over her shoulder. "I'm not into girls."

Buck caught up to walk beside her. "I see. You've already explored that with some lucky gal and now you know for certain it's not your thing."

Already explored? "Well…"

"No, I understand. Once you try something, you know for sure whether you're into it or not. You say you're not into girls, so you've clearly tried it before."

"Not exactly."

Buck placed an arm across Honey's waist, again effectively stopping her. "Wait a second. You think you're not into girls, but you've never tried it?" Her voice was full of curious incredulity.

Honey's ears burned hot. "I just never thought much about it." She shrugged, eyeing the stone path, and tucked another loose lock of hair behind her ear.

Buck gasped like she had an epiphany. She took Honey's hands. "Maybe that's why you're here. Maybe that's why we're both here."

Honey smiled. She liked how cheerful Buck glowed, a faint aura of glitter around her face. She shivered at the possibility, not sure if she was scared or full of anticipation.

Buck squeezed her hands. "You said you're in this wonderland to find out who you are, right?"

"Yes." Honey gulped.

"What if finding out who you are means making love to a woman? Maybe you'll discover a side of you that you never knew existed."

Honey giggled. "I don't know."

"Come on, Honey. You want to be treated like a queen, right?"

She looked away, not seeing the forest all around. "Well, yes."

"Why not let me show you what it's like to be treated like a queen?"

Honey shrugged. Her stomach fluttered with butterflies.

"Come on, Honey. What if the whole reason you're here is to find out Jack isn't the right person for you and that you need to find the right woman, not the right man?"

Honey toed the earth. "I don't know about that. Jack is a great guy. Besides, what if it turns out I truly am not into women, and Jack was the right man all along?"

"Then you'll know for sure. Isn't knowing better than not knowing?" Buck squeezed her hands.

Warmth shivered up her arms.

She thought about the blind man. How he helped

her buzz with sweet voices, reminding her how much she deserved to be seen, adored, treasured, loved, and cherished. Deserving was one thing. The question was, could she *let* herself be adored and cherished? Could she let herself be treated like a queen? Perhaps it was time to put that to the test.

"Come on, Honey. You know what they say." Buck stroked her hair.

"What?"

"What happens in the Forgotten Forest stays in the Forgotten Forest."

Honey scowled. "I've not heard that particular expression."

Buck shrugged. "Yeah, neither have I. But it makes sense doesn't it? Perhaps we'll forget what happened in the forest once we leave. Maybe that's partly why they call it the Forgotten Forest." Buck smiled broadly, the invitation in her warm gaze and firm grip on her hands.

Honey smiled. Buck's enthusiasm was contagious. She wanted to give in to Buck's request and let those butterflies in her belly fly free. She stared at the woman who glowed in front of her.

Buck inched closer to her, so their faces were inches from each other. "Have you ever kissed a girl?" she whispered.

Buck's breasts nearly touched her own. Heat rippled from Buck's body.

"No," Honey whispered back, her breathing

uneven.

Buck leaned in and kissed her. Her lips were tender.

Lips upon lips, Honey inhaled the tenderness.

Buck leaned back. "You even taste like honey."

Honey laughed. Goosebumps prickled her arms.

Buck put her arms around Honey, warm and comforting. "Let me treat you like the queen you are. Come." Buck took her hand and led her to a tree. She released Honey's hand, sat on the ground and leaned against the tree. "Come sit on my lap facing me." Buck smiled up at her.

Honey considered the consequences. She realized that dreams didn't have any.

Buck raised her eyebrows, a look that said, *What are you waiting for?*

Honey hitched her skirt and straddled Buck, sitting upon her thighs.

"Perfect. Comfy?"

Honey nodded. *If feeling as nervous as a performing wallflower with stage fright is 'comfy,' then yeah. I'm on a cushy cloud.*

"Good. Now, you and I are going to uncover who you are. We'll explore those very things that make you deserve to be a queen. The more I understand you, the more I can respect you. The more I respect you, the more my affection for you will be sincere. And the more sincere I am, the more accepting you'll be of my affection."

That made sense. Alice blew out a deep breath. "What do I need to do?"

Buck stroked Honey's hair. "Answer my questions." Breast to breast, Buck said, "A queen understands her quest. Her quest is a combination of three things, that which she is passionate in doing, that which she is skilled at, and that which her subjects desire most. Let's start with your passions. What do you enjoy doing?"

Honey gazed up at the breathing leaves to think on the question. "I enjoy drawing."

"A love for pictures." Buck kissed the crook of her neck. The gentle kiss warmed Honey's heart.

"I enjoy telling stories."

"A love for tales." Buck nibbled her ear. Honey closed her eyes to let the lovely feeling of appreciation wash across her skin.

"I enjoy singing."

"A love for music." Buck's kiss to her cheek added to the deliciousness of Buck's fingertips tracing circles on her back.

Honey's breathing deepened. Each kiss felt like appreciation for all Honey enjoyed. "I enjoy riddles."

"A love for wit." A kiss closer to Honey's mouth. Honey's heart beat faster.

"I enjoy reading."

"A love for the written word." Buck kissed Honey's lips. Honey tingled. It was as though Buck knew just what she needed, more than Honey knew herself.

Buck licked her lips. "You are so sweet."

Was it wrong to go through with this? Jack was her boyfriend, after all. But how can one be cheating in a dream? Still, Honey felt compelled to keep Jack in the conversation.

"I enjoy Jack's jokes."

Buck pulled her head back and eyed Honey. Was Buck upset that Honey mentioned Jack? By that smirk on her face, she didn't seem to be.

"A sense of humor." Buck smiled and stroked Honey's hair. "All right." Buck put her arms around Honey's shoulders. "If you want to involve Jack in this, then let's go deeper. Do you enjoy it when Jack kisses you?"

"Yes." Honey expected that to end this crazy lesbian session. "Very much."

Buck kissed her full on the mouth. Surprised at the kiss, Honey felt her entire body flush hot and blush. Was that even possible? Honey moved her hands about the air, not sure where to put them.

"Do you enjoy it when he feasts between your legs?" Buck kissed the other side of her neck and cupped Honey's pussy through the fabric of her dress.

Honey stiffened. "Yes." She couldn't believe Buck was touching her there. *Should I stop this?*

"Do you enjoy sucking his cock?" She stroked Honey's mound and kissed her shoulder.

Honey dropped her arms and let her head rest against Buck. "Yes." Her body was a warm happy rag doll under Buck's expert touch.

"Do you enjoy drinking his cum?"

Honey didn't answer. Her body hummed. Buck stirred her desire. She could only focus on that.

"Well then," Buck removed her hand from between Honey's legs and reached for the tie behind Honey's neck. "Now we know what you enjoy, let's find out what you're good at."

Buck tugged at the string, baring Honey's shoulders to the lovely forest air. "You like to draw. Are you good at it?" She caressed Honey's shoulders.

Honey blushed. "Not as good as my sister." Honey pretended to be focused on their conversation. She didn't want to let on how her nipples ached for Buck's touch. "It's funny. I can't remember my sister's name, nor anyone's name in my family. I can't even remember what they look like. But I remember my sister being an amazing artist. Isn't that funny?"

Buck stared engrossed at Honey's neckline above her breasts. "You're lucky. I can't remember anything." She traced the skin right above the neckline of Honey's dress. "So not an artist then. How good are you at telling stories?"

Buck tugged down the dress over Honey's breasts. Honey's heart drummed. Buck's eyes widened at the sight of Honey's bare chest. Honey's nipples pebbled and she couldn't turn away from Buck's lustful gaze.

"I seem to remember a lot of people liking my stories," Honey said, her voice deeper and softer than she intended.

Buck peered up from her admirings and smiled. "Yeah?" She cupped Honey's breasts and gently massaged them. "So you're a story teller."

Honey breathed deep into the welcome nuzzle of Buck's warm hands. "Yes. I mean, ... I suppose."

Buck stroked her hair, meeting Honey's gaze. "See? We're discovering more about you already."

Honey felt some of the butterflies release. Buck's kind smile helped her relax.

"Are you good at singing?"

"It sure seems that way in the shower," Honey laughed, her breasts jiggling in Buck's warm palms.

Buck smirked. "But others don't seem to think so?"

"Not really."

Buck traced circles around one of Honey's nipples. Honey bit her lip at the pleasure peaking at her breast.

"So, not a singer." Buck traced the other nipple. "How good are you at solving riddles?"

Honey sat up on Buck's lap, eager to answer. "I'm really good with riddles. I figure out the answers to riddles all the time. I have a bunch of friends, I can't remember their names or what they look like, but they're always trying to stump me with riddles." Honey laughed, joy bubbling up at the pleasure of it all. "And they keep getting annoyed at how I solve them all the time."

Buck squeezed her breast.

Honey gasped, at the touch and the realization. "That's probably why I'm so good with math, too! I can solve all sorts of logic problems."

Buck embraced her, hugging her against her clothed body.

"Is something wrong?" Honey asked.

"Not at all. You're just very cute when you're eager to speak." Buck pulled back from the hug. "So you're good at solving riddles and math. You didn't mention math as one of your passions. Do you enjoy math?"

Honey scrunched up her face. "Not at all."

"Okay," Buck chuckled. "So since you don't enjoy it, we'll ignore that side of you. No point in pursuing something you're skilled at if you don't like doing it."

Honey nodded. That made sense.

Buck smiled and caressed her bare arms. "You said you like reading. That's not exactly a rare skill, so let's move on."

Honey breathed in the delicate touch of Buck's fingertips along her arms, Buck seemed to truly care about her.

Buck glided her fingers along the sides of Honey's breasts. "You said you like jokes, so you have a sense of humor. How good are you at telling them?"

"I don't think I'm very good."

"Try it out. Tell me a joke."

Honey furrowed her brow and soon came up with one. "So there's this guy and he's depressed all the time. First he goes to a therapist and says, 'Doc, I'm always so depressed.' The therapist says, 'Maybe it has to do with something in your past.' But the therapist can't figure out what's bothering him. So the therapist says, 'Maybe what you need is some medicine. Go see a psychiatrist.' So the guy goes to a psychiatrist and says, 'Doc, I'm always so depressed.' And the psychiatrist says, 'Maybe it's a chemical imbalance.' So they try all kinds of medicine on him but nothing seems to work. So the psychiatrist says, 'Maybe what you need is some wisdom from a shaman.' So the guy climbs up a huge mountain to meet with the shaman. Eight weeks later he gets to the top of the mountain and finds the shaman and says, 'Shaman, I'm always so depressed. I've seen a therapist and he said it hasn't anything to do with my past, I've seen a psychiatrist and he said it hasn't anything to do with the chemicals in my brain. So what could it be, Shaman? Why am I depressed all the time?' And the Shaman says, 'Your depression is your lifestyle. You should join a Sado-Masochism community.' "

Honey waited for Buck to laugh.

Buck said nothing, just gazed at her as if expecting more.

"The guy was sad all the time," Honey explained. "So the shaman told him to make it his lifestyle and become a sadist."

Buck stared with a blank expression. The nearby leaves inhaled and exhaled in the silence.

Honey explained further. "A sad-ist?"

"Okay, so you're not a comedian," Buck said. "Now let's get to the good stuff. You said you enjoy having sex."

Honey shrugged. "Who doesn't?"

"Yes, but are you good at it?"

Honey remembered something about how troubled her sex life with Jack had been. "I don't think so."

"So perhaps being a prostitute is out of the picture." Buck laughed. "So far we have a few things you're both passionate about and skilled at. Telling stories and figuring out riddles." Buck's eyes widened and she clasped Honey's hands. "What about writing? If you're good at telling stories and like it, would you like writing?"

Honey nodded. "Yes, I think so. I've considered writing down a few of my dreams lately and turning them into stories?"

"Sexy stories?" Buck winked.

Honey smirked. "I suppose they could be."

"Then that leaves one final space to explore. People's needs." She placed her hands on Honey's knees under her dress. "You're good at riddles. Do you think many people are in dire need of hearing riddles?"

"I don't think so."

"Nor do I." Buck placed Honey's arms around her shoulders.

Honey clasped her hands behind Buck's neck, eager for the next discovery.

Buck trailed her fingers along Honey's legs, hitching Honey's dress higher. "What about writing? Are people in dire need of reading stories?"

Honey's heart pumped harder again. "I know *I'm* always in need of reading."

"Yes," Buck ran her hands up and down along Honey's bare thighs. "I believe many men and women would love to read your stories. So tell me—" She put an arm up around Honey's shoulders and with her other hand, cupped Honey's naked mound. "What would you write about?" Buck's hand under her dress felt comforting and arousing at the same time.

"My dreams, I suppose."

"Yes," Buck leaned in to whisper in her ear. "People would love to read about your dreams." Her fingers spread open Honey's folds. "What are your dreams about? Do you dream of Jack touching you here?"

Honey breathed the chocolaty air deep into her lungs. "Yes."

"What else do you dream about?"

"The chocolaty air," Honey managed to say. "The breathing leaves, the crumpet stones."

Buck's finger circled the tip of her cleft. "What else?"

Honey shivered, tingles from her core tickling across her bare skin. "The honey be's, the garden with Jack and… the neighbor whose name I forget."

"You dream of Jack?"

"Yes." Honey closed her eyes.

"Will you write about him? The way he looks?" Buck's circles on her clit made her muscles clench. She dripped her desire.

"Yes," she breathed.

"They way he touches you? The way he penetrates you?" Buck slipped a finger inside.

Honey moaned. "Yes."

"Will you write how he lavishes your nipples with good, strong licks? The way he pumps himself inside of you?" She pushed two fingers in and out of her.

Honey tilted her hips to give Buck better access, the pleasure swirling around inside her muscles clenching, grabbing for more.

"Will you write about sucking on his cock? Licking him up and down until he comes down your throat?"

Honey could almost taste Jack's salty cum in her mouth. She swallowed. "Yes."

"Will you write about everything you learned? How good it feels to have a cock in your mouth, your pussy, your ass? Will you add a nice twist to your story?" Buck twisted her fingers inside of Honey, soaking them in Honey's wet lust.

Honey raised her hips higher and clenched her fists around Buck's dress. She squeezed herself around Buck's fingers and squealed.

"Will you write about me, Honey? The way I'm helping you find your best pursuit? The way I hold you and adore you? The way I have you squirming on my hand?"

Honey rose and sank deeper onto her fingers, releasing a groan. "I will."

Buck thrust at Honey's sopping entrance, fast, in and out, quicker and quicker. "You must write a happy ending, Honey," she panted. "One that will have the fingers of your readers covered in their own cream."

"Yes," Honey moaned, eyes closed and head back, sucking in the chocolaty air and the swirls of stories and their climaxes mounting inside her.

"You must give your readers a delicious story, Honey." Buck pounded harder and faster and Honey cried out and shook upon Buck's fingers, clenching and releasing, a dream upon a dream spilling its river out onto the future pages of readers' own fingers.

The wind slowed. The leaves whispered to stillness. Honey caught her breath.

"You must include that happy ending, Honey." She placed her fingers in Honey's mouth for Honey to taste herself. "Because everyone loves a good story."

Honey licked Buck's fingers. Her essence tasted like tarts, the subject of a wonderful story.

Her body shuddered with pleasure, a wonderful "the end."

Moments later, Honey squirmed and stretched. She sucked in the delicious chocolaty air, relaxed and satiated as a kitten with a full belly of milk and cookies and marshmallows and joy. She stood up and raised her hair up to expose her neck. Right on cue, Buck also stood and helped her slide her dress over her breasts and tied the strings at her neck.

Buck held out her hand. "Let's continue down this path."

Honey took her hand. "Let's find a way out of the Forgotten Forest."

Buck smiled and nodded.

But something nagged at Honey. She frowned.

"How do you feel?" Buck asked.

"Like I've just been treated royally." Honey smiled and nodded. "Thank you."

"But something seems to be troubling you. What is it?"

"It's just that you and I did something... just now... and I liked it, but does that mean—?"

Buck laughed. "Relax. You're not a lesbian."

"How do you figure?"

"The whole time you were enjoying being treated

with love and tenderness. It didn't have to come from a woman. It could have come from a man and you would have loved it for the same reason. And that name you came up with for me? Buck? I think it was a lot easier for you to enjoy experiencing getting fingered by someone named Buck than a Clarissa or a Wendy."

Much of what Buck said rang true. She seemed very confident that Honey wasn't a lesbian. "Is there anything else that makes you think I'm not a lesbian?"

"Honey, if you were a lesbian, you'd have had your hands all over me."

Honey laughed. "I suppose so."

Buck squeezed Honey's hand. "We found out your best path to pursue. You're a story-teller and should write your stories down for the world to enjoy."

Honey breathed that in. It helped, knowing what she was good at, what she loved doing, and what the world would appreciate her for. Yes. Now Honey felt she deserved to be treated like a queen.

Honey shook her head. "Wait. What about you, Buck? Shouldn't we find out what kind of person you are?"

Buck shrugged. "I'm not concerned. For some reason I feel comfortable with who I am, as though whatever my life is outside of these woods, it's a life I already appreciate living."

Honey nodded and smiled.

Then Honey saw something shift in the light up ahead. She pointed. "Is that a clearing?"

"Sure looks that way. Maybe it's the end of the Forgotten Forest."

Hand in hand, they stepped into the clearing.

A flood of images returned to her. Her name! It was Alice, not Honey.

She turned to Buck, and recognized the woman's face. Her stomach turned.

It was her sister. "Lois!"

"Alice!" Lois's face paled and she ran away, far into the clearing and out of view.

Alice's gut weighed down, sinking further and further the more she realized what she'd just done. Lord! With her own sister!

She leaned against a tree, doubled over, and vomited all over a dark powdered ground.

"Alice!" a man's voice shouted.

She turned. Jack was running to her. Alice wiped her lips dry, the taste of fire burning in her throat and mouth. Vomit still tasted bad in this wonderland.

Jack stopped in front of her. He wore clothes she had never seen before. A black, collarless button-up shirt and tight matching trousers. Did he just come from a costume ball?

Jack caught his breath. "Are you okay?"

Alice embraced him. "I don't want to talk about it. Just hold me."

Alice inhaled. Exhaled. This was the proper way

to love. Being held by Jack. He was a man, not a sister. He loved her. She loved him. This was the right way to do things.

"Alice, I need you." He pushed her back, unbuckled his belt, unzipped his pants, and yanked them down. "Now."

Jeepers creepers! Jack was fully hard. Her waist had hardly made contact with him down there. How did he get so aroused so fast?

Jack spun her around and pressed her against a tree. The tree smelled like the ocean. A buzzing vibrated on Alice's pinky. It was the ring.

The ring is supposed to guide me. But guide me how? Is this my proper path? Is this my reconnection with Jack?

Jack flipped up her dress and squeezed her bare bottom. "I need you, Alice. I need you now."

Why did it feel so good to be manhandled this way? Shouldn't it have felt wrong? This was no way to treat a queen. What if the Alice in the mirror was just being deceptive and the ring was actually misguiding her, not helping her?

Jack's moistened fingers wriggled inside her. Alice moaned her approval.

The tree snicked against her dress, pinching her shoulders and the fabric by her nipples.

Gasping at the sensation, Alice had the fleeting thought of the bark not barking like a dog, but pinching like a crab. Only fitting that the "bark" would feel like a "crab" in this mirror world.

Jack's fingers pushed in more urgently, breaking her train of thought.

Alice exhaled and squirmed. "Yes."

She reached down and, using the hand with the vibrating ring, she cupped Jack's hand coaxing him to seek inside further. Her breasts crushed against the tree nipping at her with delicious nibbles.

Jack removed her fingers from her wetness and jammed his cock into her showing just how desperate his need was for her. Alice missed this, this urgent need Jack now demonstrated. The thrill of what it was like feeling his urgency returned. Jack pounded into her, taking her in a way that felt so right but should have been wrong. He acted completely inappropriately.

She didn't care anymore and let the pleasurable sensations take over. Cupping herself, she felt him slide between her fingers. She positioned the vibrating ring over the perfect spot for those vibrations to do their work.

The sensations that mattered weren't from the delicious feeling of being impaled by a cock.

It was Jack.

Jack needed her. He had to have her. He took her. He claimed her.

Lord, it felt so good to be needed in such a raw way.

His cock pumped her as if driving the point home. She mashed against the oceanic-smelling tree, her nipples pinched by the bark with each push. The ring vibrated its consent, guiding her closer to Jack, finding her fulfillment by pushing her pleasure higher.

"Yes," Alice whispered.

Jack reined in her arms behind her back, pinned her against the tree, and shoved himself deeper into her.

She moaned. The way Jack took her arms showed how his need for her heightened. Jack, the one she loved so much, was helpless to stop himself. He desired her, he ached for her, he demanded to have her. Her power over him made her giddy.

His thrusts came harder and faster, penetrating her deeper. Now the pleasure also came from how amazing his cock felt inside her. He had never been this rough with her. He had never been so far inside of her, either.

The mixture of his musk and her tart scents wafted. With each thrust, the sounds of her dripping pleasure smacked like lustful lips awaiting their dessert.

Harder and faster, Jack rammed into her, stretching her and filling her with his incessant demand for more of her. He pushed her higher and higher, taking from her all she could give until even the very ground she stood on seemed removed from her and she was floating to her peak.

Higher and higher, she floated, giving all of herself to Jack, letting him take everything he desired from her. He pushed her higher and higher to her peak.

At last, she arrived.

She clenched and shuddered. He yelled out her name and slammed his hips in a final thrust against her. Alice spasmed around him as he throbbed and splashed inside her.

She shook and sailed down from her orgasm.

Whoa. Alice didn't think she had felt anything that amazing before.

Jack slipped out from her, helped her stand upright, smooth down her dress, and kissed her in a long, lingering, passionate kiss.

Then he hugged her, warm, strong, and gentle.

What did she and Jack just do? It wasn't lovemaking, lovemaking was gentle and tender. It wasn't a violent molestation, either. She felt completely consensual in the act. But something about it seemed improper. It was wrong, even though it felt so right.

She held Jack tight and let the minutes pass in the afterglow of whatever it was that just happened.

Alice walked beside Jack, his arm around her waist. She breathed in the hot, cinnamon air.

She must have been arriving at the next square. That was why the air smelled different and the dirt seemed to be chocolate powder, no crumpets anywhere.

What had Queen Carol said about coming to this square?

Forget yourself and shame yourself,
Decide to cherish or despise yourself.

Alice knew quite well what the first line meant. She had forgotten who she was in the Forgotten Forest and became intimate with Lois. How shameful, indeed.

"Something is troubling you," Jack said.

Alice could see no way around it. She had to tell Jack something even if it wasn't the whole truth. "I traveled through the Forgotten Forest and forgot my name. Now I remember my name, and I even discovered what I'm good at, but I still feel like I don't know who I am."

"I'll tell you who you are. You are mine, and no one else's. You are the one who pleases me and gives me what I want, and what I need. When I want it, and when I need it. Everything you do is what I want you to do. If you do something good, I deserve the credit. If you do something wrong, I am responsible."

Alice stopped and stepped away from Jack. "Whoa, whoa, whoa. Wait a second. Are you saying I have to do everything you say?"

"Not at all. I'm saying everything you do for me is what I appreciate about you, and your decision of when to do them for me is what I appreciate most."

Alice let it sink in. She liked what she heard. "But

what about all that stuff you said about you taking the credit for what I do."

"Now that I have you, it is my responsibility to make sure you recognize all the good you've done, and appreciate it. If you realize the good you've done, I deserve the credit."

Alice scrunched up her nose. The words didn't smell right.

"Look at it this way," Jack said. "The same is true for anything you do wrong. I must take the responsibility."

"Even for my past?"

"Especially for your past. Not for what happened, but for how you feel about it. You are with me now, and I'm responsible for how you feel about yourself. You stole a cracker out of the cracker cupboard when you were five? I love you for it. You spent your past thinking you were ugly and a chore? That past has made you who you are today. And if you now know how much I desire you and crave you, then you must also know that your past had everything to do with that. All those years of feeling bad about yourself in the past shaped you into the woman I so admire."

Alice rubbed the chills at her arms. The words sounded pretty enough to her ears, but could Jack really do what he claimed? Could he make her feel good about anything she was ashamed of?

Alice spoke quietly. "What if I... did it with my

sister?"

Jack took in a deep breath and let it out. He took her by the hand. "How do you feel about it?"

Alice couldn't meet his eyes. "Ashamed." Her stomach hurt.

"Why?"

Now that was a stupid question. "Sisters aren't supposed to do it."

It was hard waiting for how Jack would respond.

He spoke softly. "Is that your choice of morality or someone else's?"

Alice scowled. "What do you mean?"

"If sisters do it, do you think it's wrong?"

She rolled her eyes. "Of course."

"Who gets hurt by it?"

Alice twirled a lock of hair, taking in another breath of the cinnamon air.

Jack shrugged. "It doesn't matter. What matters is you think it's wrong. Why did you do it if you thought it was wrong?"

"Well, this was in the Forgotten Forest. I didn't know she was my sister at the time it happened."

"But she knew you were hers?"

"No, but…"

"Then what's the problem?"

Alice sighed, not really sure what to say.

Keeping his hand in hers, Jack stepped closer to her. "Would you read a book about a man and a woman coupling?"

Alice crinkled her nose. She shrugged. "I might."

"And what if that man and woman were brother and sister?"

"Certainly not!"

"What if you found out after you read the coupling scene that they were siblings? Would that disqualify any arousal you felt before you learned the truth?"

Alice toed the earth, as though expecting to find the answer underneath the chocolate powder.

"Listen, Alice. If you feel shame, that's fine. My job in your life is to show you that what you feel now about what you've done in the past is your choice. You can choose to feel good about your decisions if you want, or you can choose to let your past mistakes guide you on your future path. I'm here to help you choose. If you want that."

Alice nodded. "I want that."

"Yes. I know you do."

> *Forget yourself and shame yourself,*
> *Decide to cherish or despise yourself.*

Alice let Jack take her down the path further into the square.

How I feel about my past is my choice. And every bit of my past has been necessary to make me who I am today.

14. Two Brothers

Two brothers, your lover, opposing each other.
You wish to know one, but don't know the other.

Square Four

"**L**ET'S rest here." Jack's words sounded more like a command than a suggestion, a command Alice was happy to obey.

Wiping the sweat off her forehead, she sat on the dirt.

Jack squatted in front of her. "I'm going to set off for a bit, but I'll be right back, okay?"

"Where are you going?"

"To the nearby messenger. I'll have him send

word of your approach to the final square. That way, everyone can prepare for your coronation if you choose to be a queen."

Alice loved that exciting thought. A coronation, just for her. She nodded.

Jack smiled. "Yes, I thought you might like that. I'll return shortly."

He clasped her head and mashed his lips against hers in a firm and passionate kiss. She met his fire with her own. Lord, just that kiss made her insides drip right out of her.

Jack broke the kiss and charged into nearby woods, a separate area from the Forgotten Forest.

Alice wanted to forge ahead and get to the final square, but running away from Jack may upset him. And upsetting Jack could incite him to wake her up. No. She needed to keep Jack calm and happy, so she waited for his return.

Voices buzzed around her. *You will be adored. You will be loved. You will be cherished. You will be seen.*

Those honey be's around her were right. As soon as she became a queen, everyone would adore her and admire her. She would gain the regal confidence she needed to present herself to the true Jack, the one outside this dream. Jack would see her and give her his full attention.

She sat down and trailed her fingers through the dirt, forming stripes in the shape of rainbows. She knew more about herself now than she did before entering the mirror world. She was a storyteller. She loved telling tales. She was good at it. And everyone loved a good story.

She licked two of her fingers, swirled them in the dirt, raised them to her lips and licked off the sweet chocolate powder. She inhaled the cinnamon air.

This square tasted wonderful.

Jack stumbled out of the woods. He waved to Alice, a goofy grin on his face. So cute.

Jack ran up to her, stopped at her feet, and bowed. "Your Majesty."

Alice laughed. "I'm not a queen yet. I'm just a pawn."

"Nevertheless, it is my duty to treat you like a queen, do your every bidding, and please you in every way possible."

Alice eyed him through the corner of her eyes and grinned. "Hmm. I like the sound of that."

Jack's shirt looked different. This one had a collar, unlike the one he wore before.

"Did you change shirts?"

"No, my love. Would you like me to?" He stepped to a tree and jumped, yanking on the nearest branch. A heavy wave of water spilled out from the tree, along with a heap of wet shirts and black crabs snapping their claws.

"Lord!" Alice cried. "What kind of tree is that?"

"A sea-shirt tree." Jack bent over and pulled his shirt off his torso. He straightened, tall, muscles rippling across his chest. "All the shirts are wet, but the day is hot enough to wear them comfortably."

Alice caught her drool from slipping out the side of her lips. She'd never tire from seeing Jack's fine, ripped abdomen, and bulging biceps.

Jack picked up a shirt from the pile and wrenched out the excess water.

The crabs migrated back up the tree and molded into the bark. How about that? A sea-shirt tree. It reminded Alice of the Mad Hatter's tea-shirt, because their names sounded so similar.

Jack tugged a loose, short-sleeved white shirt over his head. He posed with his arms out. "How's this."

She liked how Jack's muscles remained visible as the wet shirt clung to his pink body. There were words on the front of the shirt: "*Ceci n'est pas une chemise.*"

Alice pointed to the words. "That's not a shirt."

"Don't like it? All right then." He slipped the shirt off and pulled out a black vest. "Let's try this."

Alice's legs itched to hop up and scram to the last square. She fought the urge, and let Jack take the lead. The last thing she wanted was to wake up prematurely by upsetting Jack.

Jack laced his arms through the sleeves, epaulets with golden fringes sat atop his shoulders. Alice recognized the costume. The short vest merely covered his ribs. She admired his flat stomach. Her fingers tingled to caress his skin.

Jack struggled with the front of the vest. "It's too short. It won't close."

She pictured what Jack would look like in the full costume and squeezed her thighs together. "All you need is some matching tight pants and a red cape, and I'll come charging at you."

Jack scowled. "That doesn't sound very nice." He turned to the pile of shirts. "Let me try this one."

He changed into a skin-tight red shirt with long sleeves. The edges at the wrists and the circular neckline had some futuristic-looking gold lining and there was an icon on his tit, it looked like a golden-foiled footprint of a deer.

"Do I look like a man who goes boldly wherever he chooses?"

"No. That just looks ridiculous." Alice brushed the idea of it away with her hand. "You're better off without a shirt."

"As you wish." Jack peeled off the silly red shirt.

Alice licked her lips. She enjoyed the view.

He sat beside her. "What would you like me to do?"

"Just kiss me, you goof."

Jack gave her tender kisses to her lips, as though making sure she was content with each kiss.

"May I stroke your hair?" he asked.

"Of course." Alice leaned in to his loving fingers combing through her hair.

She considered telling Jack how much she wanted

to leave. Perhaps he'd agree to it. After all, hadn't he expressed his wish to please her? But the very things that pleased her didn't necessarily please him also. He might get dismayed by her request and end her adventure too soon. Alice lay back onto the ground and closed her eyes.

"May I massage your feet?" Jack asked.

"Please do."

Why was Jack asking her permission? Sure she appreciated the respect he gave her for her space, but to ask if it was okay to massage her feet? Who would say no to tha—Mmmm.

Jack's fingers squeezed into the pads of her feet and her muscles melted. His strong fingers pushed out the tension inside. She inhaled the cinnamon air and began to drift.

I'm not falling asleep, am I? Where does one go when they fall asleep in a dream? I didn't go anywhere the last time I fell asleep in this dream, back at the garden. But is it possible to have a dream inside a dream? Or does falling asleep here risk waking up in reality?

It didn't matter. She relaxed further and let her mind wander into sandy, sleepy thoughts.

"Alice!"

She jarred awake at Jack's voice. Darn it, she was just finding a nice sleep. "What?"

"I said, 'May I massage your ankles and shins?' "

He woke me to ask me permission? "Yes, of

course. Massage my ankles, shins, thighs, and further up. Anywhere would please me."

Jack's hands stilled.

She raised her head to look at him and see what the problem was.

"Anywhere?" He asked.

Alice grinned and prevented herself from rolling her eyes. "Yes, Jack. Anywhere."

"As you wish." He rolled his fingers along her ankles with soothing squeezes.

Alice laid her head back on the ground and closed her eyes. What was the riddle for this square?

Two brothers, your lover, opposing each other.
You wish to know one, but don't know the other.

Her lover was clearly Jack, so who were the two brothers?

Alice let the question slide away as Jack's fingers massaged her thighs, eking out all her concerns.

Alice breathed in uneven breaths. The slick anticipation of where his fingers were headed formed between her thighs.

His fingers reached under her dress and tentatively touched her folds. Those fingers of his teased her and traced her and roused her.

Alice writhed trying to capture his fingertips. "Please, Jack. Stop teasing me."

"What would you like me to do?"

Is he serious? Maybe he just wants to hear me say the words.

"Put your fingers inside me, Jack."

"As you wish, my love." He slowly pushed in a finger as though he were in a dark room attempting to slip a pen into its cap.

Alice growled. "Come on, Jack. Finger me with more fingers. Hard and fast."

"Yes, my love." He pushed in more fingers and thrust them quickly.

Yes. That was what she needed.

She could hear her wetness slapping with each thrust, her scent wafted mixed in with the cinnamon air. The smell of her arousal got her heart pounding, and she got into the circular chain of her own excitement triggering more desire which made her more excited.

She clenched her breasts at the height of the cycle, that moment when her desire could no longer arouse her any more. She reached that plateau and cried out, squeezing around Jack's fingers, massaging them with her clenching climax.

As the spiraling center of her mind settled down with the spiraling of her core, she let her body sink into the chocolaty powder of the earth.

"Enjoying yourselves?" A male voice asked.

Startled, Alice sat up, brushed her dress down and saw who spoke. It was Jack standing a few feet away. But then who…?

At her feet, with fingers glistening from her juices, sat another Jack.

Two Jacks?

The one standing said, "Did you enjoy pleasing her, Jackyll?"

The one at her feet nodded with that goofy grin of his. "I did, indeed."

Alice held up her hands to stop them. "Hold on a second. Jack and Jack? How come there are two of you?"

The one standing in black clothes said, "Actually, his full first name is Jackyll. I'm Hyde."

Alice tried to make sense of it.

Two brothers, your lover, opposing each other.

Alice worked on its message. *Queen Carol didn't mean that I would meet Jack and two brothers, she meant both brothers would be Jack.*

Alice recited a poem that came to mind. "Jackyll and Hyde went on a fight to fetch a medal of honor. Jackyll fell down and broke his frown, and Hyde came charging after."

Hyde chuckled and shook his head. "You call that a poem? Here's a poem:

The walrus and the dictator,
They walked along the shore.
They did not talk of many things

For each thought words a bore.
They did not savor sounds of waves,
The ocean was no more.

"Curse this blazing desert here,
And curse this sandy trend.
I wish to find me some release
But not with you, my friend."
That was when a dainty dish
Walked from the desert's end.

"Behold, dessert has come to play."
The walrus sat a spell.
"Let's greet this lovely lady and
Let's dip into her well."
To get the girl's attention there,
The walrus rang a bell.

"Hello, you two, and may I ask
What are your lovely names, sir?"
"I'm Lennon, he's Lenin," the walrus said.
"A walrus and dictator."
"That can be confusing, gents.
How do I call you later?"

"Call me John," the walrus said.
"And you can call me Dick.
Or call us by our telephones.
You can take your pick."
Lenin reached into his pants
And squeezed his mighty stick.

"I fear I'm lost," the woman said.
"I seek my fiancé."

"You're soon to marry? Wonderful!
We've brought you gifts today."
"You shouldn't have," the beauty said.
Along the sand she lay.

"We must insist," Dick said to her.
"Our presents we shall show."
They stripped their clothes, revealed their staffs,
Each one wrapped with a bow.
The lady smiled. "My thanks abound.
Please tell me where they go."

"This one goes betwixt your thighs."
"And this one 'twixt your lips."
Dick crouched above her chest and moaned
At all her lovely licks,
John raised her skirts, dipped deep inside,
And thrust into her hips.

She hummed, she writhed, she moaned and sighed,
Her head began to spin.
She lollipopped Dick's musky staff
And lapped his luscious skin.
His salty cream poured down her throat.
She shouted out, "I win!"

Dick caught his breath, bared loose her chest
And squeezed her luscious breasts.
John jacked his hammer in and out,
Her channel did the rest.
He sprayed her well, down deep inside,
And later he confessed.

"Fair lady, something you should know.
Although we fed you seed,
We took more pleasure from the giving
Than you did receive.
It's time I feed on you, my dear,
Your oyster's pearl's in need."

With that, Jack dived between her legs.
He found her pearl and lapped it.
Dick, a nipple in his mouth,
He swirled his tongue around it.
And as they fed upon her skin,
She grinned just like a bandit.

Some gasps and groans left from her lips,
Escaping to the air,
And held their hands with all the moans
And whimpers that were there.
And as she shook, convulsed, and quaked,
They could not help but stare.

When all her tremors settled down,
She thanked them with a pant.
John blushed and said, "I don't suppose
You'll tell this to your man."
"No, no, no," the maiden laughed.
"You do not understand.

"When I met you and I said,
'I seek my fiancé,'
'I'm seeking out a man to love,'
Is what I meant to say."

"In that case, miss, consider this.
Dear, wed two men today?"

"Oh, yes! I will!" the darling cried.
"You both set me aflame."
Dick placed a ring upon her finger.
John, he did the same.
She placed a ring on each of theirs,
She was a modern dame.

John's staff, it rose up once again,
And so she kindly held it.
Mrs. Lennon, Mrs. Lenin,
Whichever way you spell it,
Gave each one a lingering kiss.
With wobbly knees, they felt it.

Dick embraced her from the front,
Behind, John hugged sublime.
She felt their hard arousal and
Her naughty thoughts did chime.
But that's a story best reserved
For another time.

"Now that's a poem," Hyde explained.

Alice scraped at the edges of her thoughts trying to understand the meaning behind it. "That's the story of you two?"

Shirtless Jackyll caressed her face. "No, my love. That's the story of you two."

"Who? Me and Hyde?" Alice's confusion settled

at his touch.

Hyde stepped closer. "No, queen and slave. Princess and pea."

Alice said, "I don't understand."

"You will." Hyde smiled.

Perhaps the riddle had some answers.

> *Two brothers, your lover, opposing each other.*
> *You wish to know one, but don't know the other.*

Alice didn't see how it helped. Both Jackyll and Hyde are my boyfriend, my lover Jack. I wish to know one, but don't know the other? How could I know Jack and not know Jack?

"You look confused." Jackyll stood and offered her his hand. "Would you like to see where we come from?"

"Yes." Alice took his soft, warm hand and let Jackyll help her to her feet. "Perhaps seeing where you come from will solve this riddle."

Alice let them escort her, Jackyll in one arm and Hyde at her other, across the field.

They crossed a little bridge that took them over a creek filled with tiny cows. The cows mooed and stampeded under the bridge.

Were cows the mirror image of water? Cows? Really?

Alice shrugged. She supposed cows were about as

opposite as water as anything else.

"We're getting near," Jackyll whispered in her ear. "Be very quiet."

She wanted to giggle at how his breath tickled her ear, but she managed to stifle the urge.

Even Hyde stepped quietly, the man who just a few hours ago took her in a rough and raucous manner.

In moments, they came upon a man sleeping against a tree. Now that was definitely Jack. His jeans and denim shirt, the crow's feet at his eyes. Everything looked identical to Jack, just as she'd seen him that morning. It had to be the real man.

Jackyll whispered, "He's dreaming of us."

Alice glanced between Jackyll and Hyde. "He dreams of you two?"

"All of us," Jackyll said.

Alice scowled. "He's dreaming of me too?"

"Yes," Hyde whispered. "In fact, you're just a figment of his dreams. You wake him up and you'll disappear."

She giggled. "Impossible."

"Shh." Hyde closed his eyes and nodded. "It's true, Alice. We all exist because of him."

Hyde was being serious. Jackyll and Hyde actually believed they were figments of Jack's dream.

Alice stepped closer to the sleeping Jack.

Hyde hissed, "Don't wake him."

Alice shook her head. "I won't."

Jack breathed slow, deep breaths. His slumbering form looked so peaceful.

Alice leaned in and whispered to sleeping Jack, "Do you have any idea how much you occupy my every thought? Do you have any idea how much control you have over me? How much my happiness depends on you and how you treat me?" She gulped, then continued. "I am in such a troubled state whenever I'm around you, and in a hopeless state whenever I'm without you."

"Men." Hyde shrugged. "You can't live with them, and you can't make pea soup out of a file cabinet. Come. Let's go."

Alice scratched her head. Pea soup out of a file cabinet?

Hyde and Jackyll led her away from the sleeping Jack, back over the bridge of rushing cows, and into the open clearing of cinnamon air.

"He's got a hidden side, you know?" Hyde said.

"Who?" asked Alice. "Jack? The real Jack? I mean the one sleeping back there? Oh, how confusing this is."

"Yes," Jackyll said. "There's a side of him you've never seen."

Alice shook her head. "I'm sure he's told me everything. What hidden side are you talking about?"

Jackyll scowled. "Don't you think it's best if he be the one who tells you?"

"But aren't you two him?" She pointed at Jackyll and Hyde.

"Alice, Alice, Alice." Hyde patted her back. "You're not using your head. Think logically now. If we were both Jack, then who would Jack be?"

Alice frowned and said nothing. She strolled between them, holding their hands, thinking hard, trying to make sense of it all.

There were three Jacks in this Wonderland: Jackyll, Hyde, and the real Jack. Were Jackyll and Hyde from Jack's dreams, two parts of the true Jack? If so, what did that mean?

"You must think you can't please a man," Hyde said.

Alice lost her concentration. "What?"

"I said that you must think you can't please a man."

"Hyde," Jackyll said with a tone of warning. "Please excuse my shadow, my love."

Alice squeezed Jackyll's hand. "No, Jackyll. It's okay." She addressed Hyde. "I used to think that, but I don't anymore. I know now that I have what it takes to please a man."

"No, you don't." Hyde said. "You still can't get a man excited. Why, I bet you can't even get Jackyll hard."

Alice froze and released their hands. A lump in her throat formed, one she had thought she'd completely gotten rid of.

"Hyde," Jackyll warned again. "Don't say that—"

Alice raised the palm of her hand to stop Jackyll's words. "Jackyll, do you think I'm pretty?"

Jackyll gave a slight bow. "You are more stunning than any woman I've ever known."

Alice smiled coyly. Making him hard should be a breeze.

She stepped up to Jackyll, grabbed hold of his trouser's waistline, and tugged him close to her. He stumbled a bit, looking startled. She smirked.

"I can be daring when I want to be," she said, feeling a bit shy despite her bold actions.

She glared at Hyde and shoved her hand down Jackyll's pants.

Hyde gasped.

"Yes, I can be bold, too," she whispered, gazing at nothing particular.

She reached for Jackyll's cock and squeezed it.

Jackyll watched her hand and Hyde sucked in a breath.

Hyde was wrong. She knew how to please a man. She wasn't just going to make Jackyll hard. She was going to make him cum and wipe Hyde's face in it. She couldn't say this out loud though.

Alice continued squeezing him, but he remained soft. Maybe he needed a little coaxing.

Alice leaned in close to Jackyll's ear, lightly tugging at his cock. "Do I get you excited? Do you want to touch me? Squeeze my breasts? Stuff my pussy with your fingers?"

Jackyll looked deep into her eyes. "Yes, my love." Yet he was still soft.

Alice tried tugging a bit faster. "Do you want to stick your cock inside me? Pump me with your seed?"

Jackyll caressed Alice's hair gently. "It would be an honor, my love."

Through the corner of her eye, Alice saw Hyde leering and gasping like a wicked voyeur. Why wasn't Jackyll getting hard? Could Hyde have been right?

Alice rolled her fingers along Jackyll's length. "Maybe you'd like me to suck on your cock, swirl my tongue around it. Maybe you'd like to shove it in and out of my mouth until your cum spills down my throat. Would you like that? Would you like me to swallow your cum?"

Jackyll smiled with kind eyes. "Anything that pleases you, pleases me."

Hyde scrunched up his face like he was in pain.

Alice stopped her squeezing and asked Hyde, "Is something wrong?"

"Keep trying, Alice," Hyde said. "Pay no attention to me."

Alice clenched her fist around Jackyll's soft member. What was the matter with Hyde? Was he okay?

Jackyll sneered. "Enjoying yourself, Hyde?"

Hyde thrust his waist into the air, again and again, a huge bulge in his pants, and a wet spot growing at his crotch. After his strange humping dance, he doubled over leaning on his thighs.

Alice yanked her hand out of Jackyll's trousers. "Lord, Hyde. Did you just have an orgasm?"

Hyde nodded, panting, apparently too exhausted to reply.

"Hyde knows how capable you are of pleasing a man," Jackyll said, taking her arm. "He just wanted you to give him a good rub down."

"Me?" Alice scowled. "But I was touching you."

"Yes, but any stimulation I get, he feels, and any stimulation he gets, I feel."

Alice gasped. "Are you saying I just wanked Hyde?"

"Yes."

She tried to wrap her mind around that. "What if you want to, you know, please yourself?"

"We have an agreement," Jackyll said. "If one starts touching himself, the other does the same. That way, we can achieve our desired release whenever we wish."

Alice peered at Hyde. Still doubled over, he eyed her with a sheepish grin. Back by the sea-tree, Hyde seemed to have had no problem getting hard enough to take her from behind.

Alice turned to Jackyll. "Did you happen to…

stroke yourself just before you saw me?"

Jackyll scratched the back of his neck. "Uh, yeah. Why do you ask?"

Alice imagined Jackyll's strokes stimulating Hyde, and how Hyde suddenly needed to take her at the sea-tree.

Alice tingled deep inside at the memory.

Taking her against the tree was Hyde's way of returning the favor for Jackyll. Jackyll, not Hyde, must have been the one to actually feel what it was like to be inside her.

"Jackyll, did it feel like a hand stroking you?"

"No, now that you mention it." Jackyll wrinkled his brow. "It felt rather moist."

Alice gave Hyde a hard stare. That sheepish grin of his returned.

Alice shrugged. "Enough of this. I need to continue on my journey to become a queen."

Hyde approached her, still a bit out of breath. "I apologize for the deception, Alice. And I support any decision you make. Believe me, I do." He placed a hand on her shoulder and gave her a stern look. "But you don't want to be a queen."

Alice jerked her head back, as if she had just been slapped.

Jackyll gently placed a hand on her other shoulder. "How can you say that, Hyde? Of course she wants to be queen. That's the whole reason she's here."

Hyde crossed his arms. "Jackyll, is she here to become a queen or to learn what it means to become a queen?"

Jackyll rolled his eyes. "What's the difference? She won't know what it means unless she becomes one."

Hyde shook his head in disagreement and let out an exasperated sigh.

I must stop this bickering or else they may get upset and, if Queen Carol was correct, I could wake up without finishing the dream.

Alice put her hands on her hips. "Gentlemen, I love you both, but what I want is up to me, and no one else."

Hyde stepped close to Alice, his minty breath against her cheek. "If Jackyll and I get into a fight, will you come between us?"

"Of course."

"It means having to turn your back on one of us."

"If I must." Alice shivered. She didn't want these two Jacks to get angry and fight.

"Excellent." Hyde nodded and said to Jackyll, "Let's fight."

"Sounds good to me," Jackyll said cheerfully.

Hyde grabbed Jackyll and the two wrestled against each other in each other's arms.

Alice grimaced. If they got angry and fought each other, that could put her in danger of waking up, but it was hardly a fight if they both happily agreed on "fighting."

Hyde grunted, "First to orgasm wins." He threw Jackyll to the ground and climbed on top of him, clamping a hand on Jackyll's crotch. He grinned as he stroked Jackyll over the fabric of Jackyll's trousers.

Jackyll pushed him off, rolling until he had a hold of Hyde, pinning Hyde's hands to the earth. Jackyll ground his hip against Hyde's crotch. Hyde struggled to escape. Jackyll rubbed his hip along Hyde's cock faster, moaning at the pleasure his own must have been feeling.

Alice smirked at the show. An undeniable trickle formed between her thighs.

Jackyll's eyes rolled to the back of his head in ecstasy. Hyde wriggled out from under Jackyll's body, shoved Jackyll to the ground, and sat on Jackyll's face, facing the rest of Jackyll's body. Hyde unbuckled Jackyll's belt, unbuttoned the waist button, unzipped his fly, and snuck a hand inside.

They may have been acting ridiculous, but Alice wasn't about to stop them. Her plan was to enjoy the show. Hitching up her skirt, she licked three fingers and set out to follow her plan.

Hyde had his hand down Jackyll's pants and was yanking rapidly. Hyde moaned.

Alice's knees buckled. She plunked herself on the ground, her dress pushed up at her waist and her legs bent wide open to give her fingers better access to her nubby pleasure.

On his back, Jackyll reached for Hyde's pants on his face, and working the front of his trousers, managed to free Hyde's cock.

Alice gasped. The thing looked ready to pop. She shouldn't have been too surprised. By the way Hyde's hand yanked furiously inside Jackyll's trousers, the proof of his handiwork showed on Hyde's own cock. Hyde must have known exactly what felt right.

Alice's heart pounded at the two glorious erections and the men working them so beautifully. She pushed two fingers inside herself.

Jackyll tugged down on Hyde's cock and sucked on the tip. Jackyll arched his neck and managed to get more of Hyde's shaft down his throat. Moans escaped Jackyll's lips, though his mouth was full of Hyde's cock.

Jackyll must have been moaning over the sensations his mouth was creating.

Lord! I've never seen a man give himself a blow job before.

Alice thrust her fingers in deeper and faster, spurred on by the excitement formed by Jackyll and Hyde's wrestling.

Hyde growled at Jackyll, "Oh no you don't." He clamped his free hand around Jackyll's neck and was choking him.

What in the heavens?

Jackyll gagged. His face was turning blue.

Alice popped to her feet and dragged Hyde off of Jackyll. "That's enough!"

The two men stood, their cocks at attention, pants around their ankles. Alice stood between them.

Hyde huffed, "You said you would come between us if we fought."

"Yes," Alice said. "So I have."

"Not completely," Hyde said. "You're between us, yes, but now you must come." He stepped close, his body against hers. She turned and Jackyll stood at her chest.

Alice gulped but didn't move. She'd planted herself between Jackyll and Hyde and was now ready for whatever came next.

Jackyll at her front, his stiffened cock to her waist. Hyde at her back, rubbing, moaning, nudging her with urgency at Alice's crevice.

Lord, was this cheating? She was with Jack. Both of him. The concept was too challenging, and too exciting, to focus clearly.

She wanted this to happen though. Her hardening nipples said so, her heavy breathing said so, her pounding heart said so. Hell, the desire spilling from between her legs practically screamed it out.

Forget the trouble of sorting out which, if either one, was Jack. The whole experience was just a dream. She had to go with it. Had to.

Hyde hiked up her skirt and by the peaking of her nipples and the spilling of her core, she felt the excitement of both men seeking their way into her. Jackyll found his way first.

Alice sighed at the pleasure of being filled.

Hyde nudged his way behind her. "Relax."

Alice found that challenging when all she wanted to do was clench tighter around Jeckyll.

Jeckyll must have sensed her difficulty because he stilled himself inside her, letting Alice adjust to the delicious sensations.

"Relax," Hyde whispered again.

She took in a deep breath of the cinnamon air, then exhaled, allowing all her muscles to let go.

Hyde pushed in. Alice sucked in a hiss of breath, squeezing and clenching at the invasion of his cock. Lord, it felt big!

Jackyll moaned.

Oh, yeah. He's the one who's feeling what it's like to be up my ass.

The delicious burn triggered a tiny wildfire escaping down Alice's legs, and across her chest and nipples, and up her neck. Lord, getting completely filled with two men desiring her, Alice pitied any woman who didn't get the chance to know how it felt. She squeezed tighter around Hyde's tip.

"Relax," Hyde said.

Alice huffed three breaths and let go.

Hyde pushed in deeper.

Alice and Jackyll cried out together. She tightened her muscles, squeezing their cocks.

"Oh, my love," Jackyll stared into her eyes gently holding her head. "You feel incredible."

Alice couldn't speak. She only smiled through her heavy breaths. Jack had such beautiful eyes. Or Jackyll. Or whoever this was.

"Alice," Hyde prompted.

She got the hint and relaxed her muscles.

Hyde pushed in all the way.

Alice bit her lip adjusting to the pain and pleasure combination, but Jackyll didn't give her enough time. He hoisted Alice up by her legs and placed them around his torso. He pushed gentle thrusts into her. Hyde greeted the thrusts with a groan, his cock feeling thicker with each shove of Jackyll's hips.

Alice took it all in. Jack in front of her. Jack behind her. Twice the Jack. Twice the attention. She desired his adoration so much, and now he filled her with twice the adoration.

Hyde pounded into her from behind. Jackyll kissed her, his gentle tongue sweet and loving. She tightened her channels, feeling them both.

Twice the Jack. Twice the attention.

Jackyll's face turned into a grimace. He was close. Tiny explosions scattered across her skin. Alice wriggled and squirmed with pleasure, no longer in control of her body. Then the orgasm shot through her. Pleasure popped through her flailing body. She screamed out for the world to hear all.

Jackyll frowned and let out a cry. She smiled as she felt him spray inside her.

Hyde held Alice up when Jackyll collapsed to the ground, breaking contact with her. Jackyll smiled, his frown now gone, and he played with his cock. Then Hyde came charging after.

Alice panted along with her men. Jackyll stroked himself faster. Hyde managed to clutch Alice's pussy and quiver his hand across her clit as he speared her hard and hot and thick and quick until he shouted and shot his cream in her ass. Alice squeezed her breasts, twisting her nipples, persuading them to join the fiery party where Hyde impaled her, and to join the seeping celebration at her pulsating pussy.

Her nipples prickled with gratitude as Hyde softened inside her.

Hyde eased her to the ground. Her legs were too shaky to function for the time being. Alice sat up, looked at each Jack, and admired how they tucked away their glistening cocks.

Jackyll crouched beside her. "You are so beautiful, my love." He laced a lock of hair behind her ear and lightly kissed her lips. His kiss was sweet, his words endearing. He stood.

Hyde pushed her to the ground. He mashed his lips against hers sending her heart pounding, from fear or excitement. She wasn't sure which. Yanking up her dress, he cupped her mound and rubbed her with desperate fingers. Alice's nipples hardened, aching to be touched.

He broke the kiss. "You turned your back to me, Alice. But I know you. You want this. You don't like the way Jackyll treats you."

Alice didn't understand. She worked to speak over the delicious waves of pleasure Hyde performed with his fingers "But I do like his ways! Jackyll treats me very well. Like a queen."

Hyde stopped his fingers. Alice stifled her disappointment.

He said, "You don't want to be a queen, Alice."

She didn't reply. Why did he keep saying that?

Hyde stood up and dusted himself off. "But I respect your choice."

Alice's pussy still throbbed with aftershocks, and her nipples desired more attention, but the arousal dwindled enough to control herself.

Hyde held out a hand to help her up. "Will you at least let me take you to the final square for your coronation?"

At last! She took his hand. "I'd be delighted."

Hyde propped her on her feet. "Excellent. Then I'll make sure everything is in proper order for you and meet you on the way to the seventh square."

"I look forward to it." Alice smiled.

Two brothers, your lover, opposing each other.
You wish to know one, but don't know the other.

Alice considered the solution to the riddle.

Perhaps Jackyll and Hyde were two sides to Jack, one she wished to know better and one she didn't know at all. The question was, which one did she wish to know and which one did she not know at all?

Droplets tapped the top of her head.

Hyde looked up. "We better leave. It will soon be raining."

Alice saw cows floating in the sky, blocking out the sun. A drop landed on her lips. She tasted it. "Milk?" It was sweeter than she remembered milk being.

"Yes," Jackyll said looking concerned. "We'll soon be in the middle of a flood of chocolate milk if we don't leave soon."

Jackyll and Hyde raced off together across the clearing and into the nearby woods. Alice sprinted after them with no path to follow, trying to catch up to them.

15. The League of Heroes and the Cage of Groans

You drip with excitement, you're wet with desire.
But not everything wet will come from a fire.

To Square Five

ALICE ducked under the cover of tall trees but couldn't find Jackyll or Hyde anywhere. Where could they have gone? Alice ventured further, on wobbly knees from her last workout with them, and with other lovely memories of them trickling down her legs.

She scanned the woods, but didn't spot them. In

the drizzle of white rain plopping through the leaves of the forest, Alice sighed and decided that she should move on with her adventure.

What was the next riddle?

You drip with excitement, you're wet with desire.
But not everything wet will come from a fire.

Alice touched her breasts. She liked the sound of that riddle.

She found a path and followed it deeper into the woods, certain by its constant forward direction that it would take her to the next square. The rain got heavier even with the cover of the trees. Something was different, though. They didn't smell like sea-trees. They smelled like they were burning. Alice examined one of the trees closely.

The leaves were high up, too high to examine them closely. They weren't breathing, though. They weren't crumpling and expanding like the leaves of the last forest. Instead, they were tan in color and made crackling sounds.

A ripping noise gave Alice just enough warning to shift out of the way of a branch that fell to her feet. She picked up the branch and studied the leaves. Toast? The leaves were pieces of toast?

She picked up the soaked tan bread and squeezed the milk out of it. "I suppose this would be milk toast."

The rain pounded and more soaked bread dropped around her.

I better get out of these woods. The rain may get me wet, but the falling toast could give me bruises.

She picked up the pace and hustled along the path, dodging the falling leaves. A few minutes later she stumbled into a clearing and bent over to catch her breath. The danger of being hit by falling toast was over. The cows had parted in the sky and the sun peeked through.

She shivered. Her dress and hair were sopping in cold milk.

Not everything wet will come from a fire.

Alice rolled her eyes. She wasn't dripping wet from arousal. She was dripping wet because of the rain.

She put her hands on her hips and spoke into the air. "Well, I hardly see how knowing that is of any use."

She puffed out a breath of frustration to blow a wet strand of hair out of her eye.

A short distance away stood a crimson palace seven stories high with odd spires. Their coiled lengths were topped with hands cupping the sky.

Could that be a queen's palace?

Though the nearby shrubs beside her were waist-high, tall green hedges as tall as her house, formed parallel paths on the grounds pointing straight to the palace. The grounds were quite well-tended. The palace must be special indeed.

Upon closer inspection, the hedges sported branches resembling arms, hands, and leafy fingers reaching upwards. The base of the hedges looked like nothing more than a collection of arms growing close together.

Still green, though.

Alice curled her toes around the grass at her feet. The grass squished between her toes. It felt good. Did the air still smell of cinnamon? She took a deep breath. No. It smelled sour, metallic. Not pleasant at all. Alice shrugged it off and focused on the good parts of this clearing.

She gazed upon the beauty of the crimson palace with its gold trim and the surrounding hedges. This was how she wanted her palace to look when she became a queen.

She shivered in her cold, damp clothes. The milky rain had drenched her dress and bra. She tugged off her dress, squeezed out the milk, and lay the dress across a squat shrub of fingers to dry. She wanted to leave on her bra, but the idea bothered her.

If only I still had my panties.

With no one around, walking in her bra and panties would have been okay. Hell, she even felt comfortable with the idea of walking around topless in her panties. But for some reason, walking with just a bra on didn't feel right.

Alice snapped off her bra and rested it on the bush of fingers beside her dress. She strolled naked toward the palace. Her bare skin sizzled warm under the sun. She padded across the grass between two walls of hedges, threading her fingers through her wet hair, separating the strands to dry faster.

Arriving at the palace, she saw a single metal door. It looked too ordinary to be a palace door, as if it had been added to the building as an afterthought. Alice turned the round handle. Locked.

Perhaps this side of the palace was the back.

Alice walked the extensive back wall and peered around the corner to make sure no one was around. She was naked, after all.

Beyond the side of the palace, far in the distance, the gardens looked much more polished and grandiose. The front of the palace must have been at the other end of the building.

Alice scurried alongside the palace. Upon approaching the opposite side, she covered her breasts with her hands, just in case people were there.

Around the next corner, she gasped. The front garden spanned acres and acres with a symmetrical layout of tall hedges, their arms and hands reached up and cupped the sky. She was alone. Not a soul in sight.

She dropped her hands to her side and jogged to the main entrance, a set of iron-cast double-doors as tall as the hedges. The doors were wide open. Above the portal, a sign displayed French words etched in stone.

Her finger buzzed. It was the ring. It vibrated against her finger with urgency. Why would the ring guide her here? Jack was nowhere. She peered inside the palace and whistled softly at the enormity of the room. The main entrance was a single hall, the left side tall wall lined with free-standing sculptures, marble statues of men. Was this a museum?

Someone moaned.

Alice covered her breasts.

It sounded like a woman in distress or arousal. It was hard to tell.

"Hello?" Alice called out.

No response. Aside from the statues, the museum was empty.

She stepped inside. The place smelled of sweat. "Hello?"

No response. Just the sound of a woman moaning. Was the moaning a recording? A fixed part of this exhibit?

Breasts cupped, Alice gulped. What kind of museum plays recordings of a woman moaning?

She rushed outside and examined the French words above the doors. She worked at translating them. They read, "La Ligue Des Héros et La Cage aux Gémissements."

The League of Heroes and the Cage of Groans? What sort of museum was this?

Alice returned inside, just past the doorway. The sounds of a single woman moaning echoed against the walls. Those moans were primal, sounding as though she were enjoying herself.

The ring on Alice's finger buzzed stronger. As much as she wanted to explore the museum, she needed to get to the final square for her coronation before waking up. But was there really any danger in waking up? There was no sign of the black knight, and Jack was nowhere to be seen. As far as where Jackyll and Hyde disappeared to, she had no idea.

Alice stood tall and relaxed her shoulders. This museum was safe from any risk of waking up, and the ring seemed to want her here.

Listening carefully she heard no indication of any other people in the museum. She dropped her hands from her breasts and soaked up the vast hall. The ceiling graced a mural depicting a beautiful woman wearing a crown and men prostrating themselves before her, worshipping her, offering her gifts of jewels and gold. Alice wanted that to be her on the throne, men bowing at her feet, adoring her.

The moaning came from the opposite end of the hall where an empty iron cage stood.

Something moved out of the corner of her eye.

Alice gasped.

Why hadn't she noticed how odd the statues behaved before? They were moving. Certainly, slow enough to hardly tell, but moving nonetheless. Each muscular man of stone continuously changed its pose with slow and fluid motions. Each new position remained a handsome pose of its own.

Alice strolled up to the first of the eight statues. Her ring hummed happily. The muscular man wearing just a loincloth carried a sword and a scowl, shifting his stance as though preparing for battle.

Alice read the plaque: "Borelius – For the queen, he slaughtered six pawns, a knight, and a bishop, clearing the way for his men to capture the witch. Long live the queen!"

Alice took one more lingering glance at the well-built Borelius. He held his sword above his head and stared off to the side at a non-existent enemy.

She moved to the next statue. A man stood, gripping a mace with a spiked ball twice the size of his head. His arm's muscles bulged bigger than any Alice had ever seen. He likely needed the strength to carry that weapon. She read the plaque: "Erelius – For the queen, he battered down the castle doors to help with capturing the witch. Long live the queen!"

The statue of Erelius wore a fierce expression. Perhaps he had just hammered down doors. He gazed high above Alice's head with a defiant look, as though daring others to stop him.

Alice wondered what he might do to her if she got in his way. She smirked at the thought.

The next statue displayed an old man in a long cloak.

The plaque showed his name to be Arelius. Borelius? Erelius? Arelius? This culture may have been skilled at building palaces and creating sculptures, but coming up with unique names wasn't one of their skills.

She read the old man's plaque: "Arelius – For the queen, he used his magic as a master wizard to break through the witch's invisible shield surrounding her throne room. Long live the queen!"

The wizard stood, knees slightly bent, his hands cupped as if swirling a fireball in front of him.

Alice moved to the next statute. She liked the looks of him, a well-built man in a loincloth, eyeing the ground with a countenance of determination. Alice positioned herself so that his gaze fell upon her, and pretended he could truly see her. If that determination was directed at her, what was he determined to do to her?

She read his plaque: "Serelius – For the queen, he ripped off the witch's robes, stripping her of her dignity. Long live the queen!"

Alice licked her lips. It sounded much more interesting to be the witch than the queen.

Is that what you would do to me, Serelius? She gazed down at her nakedness and chuckled. *I'm afraid you're a bit too late to strip me.*

The ring vibrated a bit stronger. Alice couldn't help thinking that perhaps the ring was warning her more than guiding her.

The next statue was of a man gripping a knotted length of rope up to the light as though examining it.

The plaque read: "Lorelius – For the queen, he tied up the witch. He bound her hands and feet with ropes of the strongest silk, making her powerless to move and cast spells. Long live the queen!"

Alice gazed up at Lorelius. What it must have been like for him to pin her down to the floor and tie her up! Was it really as awful as it was supposed to sound?

The next statue had Alice clenching her thighs together. It portrayed a man too handsome to have ever truly existed. He seemed to be peering straight at her. What was it about him? The muscles? The ripped abdomen? The scruff of sculpted hair on his head? Could it have been how he was completely naked, the ample length of his cock hanging freely between his legs?

Panting a little, she read the plaque: "Atrelius – For the queen, he dissolved the witch's power by making her drink his sorcery-neutralized essence. Long live the queen!"

Alice gasped. Was that what she thought it meant? The witch drank his cum? Did the witch have that magnificent cock down her throat?

Alice scanned Atrelius for what made him so gorgeous. It had to be his face. Definitely. The single raised eyebrow, the impish curl at his lip. They called to her. She wanted to taste his essence.

Glancing side to side, Alice made sure no one was around. She climbed upon the wide base of the statue to stand beside Artelius. Lord, he was a giant. Her head came up to his stomach.

She gripped his stony length. It was warm and pulsed under her palm. Her heart quickened. She gave it a squeeze and gazed up at Artelius's face.

He smiled. Her heart beat faster.

Could he feel this? Sure seemed that way.

A wicked thought pierced her mind. How did he taste?

Alice watched his face and gave his hanging cock a long lick from tip to sculpted hair. He tasted like sweat. Alice smiled at the salty taste and climbed down to the tiled floor. She sighed at the brief but pleasant connection she made.

The next statue stood with his hands fisted on his hips, a sculpted bear fur over his shoulders.

The plaque read: "Vorelius – For the queen, he braved the bitter cold weather to transport the witch to the royal castle. During the journey, he often had to share his bed with the witch to keep her from a freezing death. Long live the queen!"

Alice feasted her eyes on this bear of a man who kept the witch warm during the cold nights. Somehow, the witch's punishing capture seemed less and less of an ordeal.

She grinned and moved on down the long hallway to the next and final statue. This man wore a blacksmith's apron.

Alice read the plaque: "Etrelius – For the queen, he crafted the Cage of Groans to imprison and enslave the witch for eternity. Long live the queen!"

The statue of Etrelius stood proud with his hammer resting upon his shoulder.

So these were the League of Heroes.

Alice recited their names in her mind.

Borelius.

Erelius.

Arelius.

Sorelius.

Lorelius.

Atrelius.

Vorelius.

Etrelius.

Alice filed those men for a fantasy for a future day. The source of the moans came from an iron cage at end of the hall. Was the sound a recording at all? Or was there someone inside that cage all this time?

Alice's ring shook with earnest vibrations. Considering the situation, those vibrations were more likely a warning for Alice to beware of the witch. Perhaps when Hyde took her with such rough demand at the edge of the Forgotten Forest, the ring was trying to warn her then, as well. He had, after all, been quite brutal, the way he slammed his desire into her. It would make sense that the ring had tried to alert her of his harsh behavior. If the buzzing ring were a warning, it would be best to steer clear of the witch.

Alice turned to leave, but the moans kept her curious. What if someone needed help? What if Alice was called here by the ring to free the woman who was locked inside?

She approached the cage with cautious steps. The cage appeared empty, but Alice soon realized the bars surrounded a small pool. Inside the pool swam a naked beautiful raven-haired woman, moaning endlessly.

At first, Alice had trouble understanding what the bronze-skinned woman was swimming in. It wasn't water. It moved like sand, shifting and shaping itself around the woman's body. Then the sand changed into fingers, arms, lips, even moist tongues.

Lying on her back, the woman's flushed chest was covered with hands and fingers pulling her into the pool by her every crevice. Lips and tongues lapped at her delicate shoulders, her pert breasts, her flat stomach. The woman popped up from the pool and grabbed hold of the iron bars. She panted with her eyes closed. Lips at her copper-colored nipples shifted their shape into hands, then fingers, which dripped down her chest. The fingers turned back into lips, licking her smooth skin on the way down, then joined the rest of the pool.

The gorgeous woman opened her chocolate eyes

and saw Alice.

Was she going to plead for help? Was she going to ask Alice to release her?

Alice stared speechless, not sure what to do.

The woman chuckled as if knowing something Alice didn't. She let herself fall backward into the pool. A finger reached into her mouth and shifted into a cock. She moaned as cum spilled from her lips.

16. The Beauty Queen

To be a queen you must understand,
Every queen in the land.
Spell the word "but," not the word "and,"
To unlock the troubles a queen has at hand.

Square Five

FRIGHTENED by the caged witch, Alice raced toward the back door of the hall. It was the same metal door she had spotted when she first came upon the palace. Good. From the inside, the door opened. She slipped through and hastened outside into the sour air and sunny backyard of towering hedges. She trembled. What was that? Did Alice really just see an imprisoned witch happy with her punishment?

What had Queen Carol said about this?

To be a queen you must understand, every queen in the land. Spell the word "but," not the word "and," to unlock the troubles a queen has at hand.

There was no mention of a witch. But something else tugged at Alice's chest. How beautiful that witch was! The woman was just another reminder of Alice's imperfections. Yes, in the story Carol told her Solette was a homely and dirty woman who wasn't pretty or beautiful to anyone and then became the prettiest queen ever because she believed herself to be beautiful and loved herself and adored herself, yada, yada, yada. But that was just a story. If Alice couldn't be as pretty as a witch, how could she ever expect to be beautiful enough to be a queen?

Before Alice could speculate any further, she was startled by the sobs of another woman coming from beyond a nearby tall hedge.

Now that Alice had returned to the back of the museum, she could fetch her clothes. Luckily, they were right where she left them to dry, on the nearby waist-high shrub of arms and fingers. She donned her bra and slid her dress over her head. She sighed. They were sun-warmed and dry.

At the back of her neck, she tied the lace of her dress and walked around the hedge, following the sounds of the sobs into a field.

She crinkled her nose. The sour smell and metallic taste in the air grew fouler. She covered her nose with her palm, as if that could help diminish the acrid odors. It did, a little.

The sobbing pulled her forward. She climbed a hill and saw a grassy clearing below. In the middle of the clearing sat a crying lady in front of a cherry wood vanity mirror.

Alice recognized the woman. It was Lucy, her old classmate, the beauty queen of secondary school. Even now, a gold crown hung off the back of the chair.

Alice padded to Lucy. Close up, the crown looked tarnished with a few gems missing. The black princess dress Lucy wore was frayed and torn, hanging off of Lucy's shoulder. Lipstick was smeared across her cheek. Wide circles of eyeliner raccooned her eyes, but somehow, through it all, and through her sobs, Lucy still looked beautiful.

To be a queen you must understand every queen in the land.

So that was what Queen Carol meant. Alice had to speak with Lucy. From what Alice remembered, Lucy had been stuck up. All the girls pretended to be her friend, but hated her, and all the boys drooled over her. Alice had called her a bitch behind her back.

Seeing Lucy in shambles, the girl who had possessed everything, gave Alice a bit of satisfaction. Then Alice felt a pang of guilt for getting pleasure from Lucy's sorrow.

"Lucy?"

Alice's former classmate sucked in her sniffles and returned to applying makeup. She dabbed a brush of blush on the top of her head. "Alice, so good to see you."

"Good to see you, too." Alice watched Lucy's strange behavior.

Lucy stifled a sob. It was hard to see Lucy so sad, harder still to see her pretending not to be.

"What's wrong, Lucy?"

Lucy puffed out a chuckle and dabbed her eyes with a handkerchief. "That obvious, eh?"

Alice didn't say anything. She waited for Lucy to reveal what troubled her.

Lucy picked up some coral nail polish that had been nestled in a small pile of lingerie and lacy underwear on the vanity.

"I've always been the beauty queen." Lucy applied the nail polish to her knuckles. "People always treated me like a queen, and no one uttered a disapproving word to me. I never knew who my friends were and who was just pretending to be. Were you my friend, Alice?"

"Of course, Lucy," Alice lied. "I still am."

Lucy yelped in pain.

Alice jumped, startled, then knelt at Lucy's side. "What happened?"

"That hurt." Lucy rubbed her wrists.

Alice searched her face and body. "What hurts? What's the matter?"

"Forget it." Lucy waved it off. "I cried out in pain because I'll soon cut myself. Better to get it out of the way, right?"

Alice struggled to understand how feeling pain before getting cut was a better order of things.

"So you say you were my friend?" Lucy shook her head. "I don't know if you're lying or if you're just being nice."

Before Alice could defend her lie, Lucy put up a hand to stop her. "I'm dressed this way because I thought by making myself ugly, people would treat me like a normal person." She applied nail polish on the pads of her fingertips. "But that didn't work. Do you know how many men have said they love me just to bed me and never talk to me again?" Lucy's face hardened with a scowl and tight lips.

Alice remembered the rest of the riddle.

Spell the word "but," not the word "and," to unlock the troubles a queen has at hand.

Alice softly spelled the word to herself to see how it sounded. "B-U-T. Beauty." Beauty was the trouble Lucy had to deal with.

"You're lucky you're not a queen, Alice. You deserve to be treated with honesty." Lucy picked up a razor blade and quietly applied it to her wrists. Blood spilled out.

"No!" Alice shouted. She grabbed Lucy's wrists,

covering the wounds with her palms. "We have to stop the bleeding. What can we use to stop the bleeding?"

Lucy smiled. "I don't want to stop the bleeding. Why would I?"

"It's a bad thing," Alice said, panic clutching her heart. "If you bleed out too much it's bad."

"Don't cry, Alice. Consider how great you are. Consider how far you've come today. Consider how practical spoons are. Consider anything. Just don't cry."

Alice's gaze darted across the vanity. She spotted a package of cotton balls and grabbed them. She pulled apart the box. Cotton balls spilled all over. She grabbed a handful and pressed the cotton against Lucy's cuts. The bleeding wasn't stopping.

"It's bad," Alice muttered. She grabbed more cotton balls and squeezed down on Lucy's wrists.

"It's not bad," Lucy said.

Alice had trouble seeing through the blur of her tears.

"It's not baaad," Lucy said again.

The cotton seemed to spread up Lucy's arms, though Alice couldn't be sure. Wiping away her tears, she saw the cotton climb Lucy's shoulder.

"It's not bah-ah-ah-ad," Lucy bleated.

What was going on?

Alice rolled up Lucy's sleeves and noticed the arms changing shape. Lucy bleated and wriggled on the chair.

Lord! Lucy was a sheep!

The sheep wiggled out of Lucy's dress, and with merry bleats, darted into the woods.

17. The Mirror

While it's good to wish to grab a he-pole,
The queen will show what kind of people
Blindly follow the path she has taken,
A path of royalty much mistaken.

To Square Six

ALICE plopped into the chair in front of the vanity mirror. What had just happened? One minute she was talking to Lucy, the next she was trying to save Lucy's life. Then Lucy turned into a sheep.

Alice's gut churned from the memory of all that blood.

She picked up the hairbrush on the vanity and brushed out her long hair. The brushing helped her think.

She talked it out to herself in the mirror. "Queen Carol wanted me to speak with Lucy to learn a lesson. Being beautiful comes with a price. Big deal. So does being ugly or looking different. I bet Lucy has no idea what it means to be teased and verbally tortured just because she isn't pretty. And to grow up never getting a second glance from a boy until your boobs grow out."

Alice tugged harder at the knots in her hair.

"Lucy never had to deal with that. What was the worst she had to put up with? Boys adoring her all the time? Girls giving her gifts? Yeah, that was some price to pay, all right. I'll take it at any price. Let me go get my purse."

She sneered at herself in the mirror and set the hairbrush down. She gazed at herself in the mirror and stilled, her mind quiet enough to hear the honey be's buzzing around, whispering, "You will always be cherished. You will always be loved. You will always be seen."

Alice smiled and inhaled the allure of Jack adoring her, cherishing her, and loving her. Doing so brought out the metallic scent of blood in the air. She had to get rid of that awful smell.

A bottle of perfume was perched on the vanity. Alice picked it up and smelled the nozzle. She scowled. The perfume smelled like fried chicken.

Alice shrugged. Fried chicken smell was better than the metallic scent of blood. She squeezed the bulb and sprayed the perfume all around the mirror. The fragrance of fried chicken surrounded her. Much better.

She checked her hands where she'd applied pressure to Lucy's wounds. She still had smears of blood across her palms. She grabbed the bottle of rubbing alcohol on the vanity. That would do. Alice picked up a few cotton balls and opened the bottle bracing herself for the strong smell of alcohol. Instead, an earthy scent wafted up. It smelled like Jack.

Alice sighed and held the bottle close to her nose. She inhaled Jack's scent and smiled.

She dampened the cotton and swabbed off the blood until her palms were clean.

What was the next riddle?

> *While it's good to wish to grab a he-pole,*
> *The queen will show what kind of people*
> *Blindly follow the path she has taken,*
> *A path of royalty much mistaken.*

Alice dried her hands on Lucy's handkerchief.

Grabbing a he-pole instantly brought to mind Alice's little misbehavior with the statue of Artelius. She smirked at the naughty memory. What would be the opposite of a he-pole? A she-pole? Well, that was silly. Girls don't have such things.

Alice picked up the hairbrush again and ran it

through her hair, reciting aloud: "She-pole, she-pole, she-pole. Lucy turned into a sheep. Sheeple, sheeple, sheeple."

Alice paused, stared at her reflection without really looking, and spoke, "The queen will show what kind of people blindly follow the path she has taken. Not people, but sheeple. People blindly follow her path like sheep because of her path of royalty. She's a queen, and others want to be a queen, too." Alice scowled. Was Queen Carol saying that those who follow the path of becoming a queen were sheeple? That such a path always lead to disappointment?

She shook her head and frowned at her reflection. Her own case was different. She didn't want to become a queen in the real world, she just wanted to be treated like one.

How could being treated like a queen be disappointing?

Alice rejected the lesson. Maybe the lesson was an important one, but it didn't apply to her. Alice just wanted to be treated like a queen.

The odor of fried chicken hovered around her. It was time to set off for the next square. She set down the hairbrush and noticed Lucy's pile of lingerie and lacy underwear. By the neat pleats in the fabric, all of them appeared to have never been worn. Sifting through, she found a pair of ordinary white cotton panties. She stood and threaded her legs through and tugged them on beneath her dress.

That felt better.

"Alice? Is that you?"

Alice whipped around. "Jack?"

"Over here. Through the mirror."

She checked the vanity mirror. Instead of a reflection, she saw Jack's overlarge face peering through.

"Jack!" Alice smiled. She pressed a hand where his cheek was in the mirror, but only felt glass. "How did you get there?"

"I'm in the library. You're still stuck in the hand mirror it seems." He put a huge fingertip to Alice's hand, the glass separating them.

Alice frowned. "I wish I could just smash this mirror and crawl right through."

"Me too. I miss you, Alice."

This is just a dream. Now's the perfect time to practice asking for what I want. I just need to be careful not to aggravate him or cause him too much stress. Doing so might make him wake me up somehow.

"Jack, you know how I said I wanted you to treat me like a queen?"

Jack grimaced.

Alice reminded herself not to aggravate him. "What's wrong?"

"Now's not exactly a good time to talk about that."

Alice shook her head. "No, Jack. Now's the

perfect time."

Jack pinched the bridge of his nose. "All right, Alice. What about it?"

"I need you to give me more attention and show me that you care about me. Last year and during the summer you did all sorts of things for me, and now it's like you don't even know I'm here."

Jack raised his brows. "Alice, everyone is important. You're not more important than anyone else. Why should I treat you any different?"

"You're my boyfriend." She clenched her fists. "Don't I deserve more attention than others?"

"I have a lot of responsibilities, Alice. I can't be there for you all day everyday. You need to realize that."

"I know that, Jack. All I'm asking is for you to treat me the way you did before." Alice sat down in front of the vanity mirror and spoke softer. "It's like you've changed."

Jack sighed. "People change. I'm going to change, you're going to change, it's inevitable. You're already changing, and I accept that. Does that mean you won't accept me when I change?"

"That's not what I mean. Of course I'll accept you if you change."

He said, "The doctor's here to help with the poison, Alice."

Alice stiffened. "What?!"

Was someone poisoned? Her mother, perhaps?

Her sister? Her father was always as healthy as an ox in a vitamin shop, it couldn't have been her father.

"I hear you loud and clear, Alice. You want me to be the same guy you fell in love with."

Okay. So there's no doctor. No one's poisoned. I must have misheard him.

"But, Alice, I *am* the same guy. I have the same responsibilities, and I will always be busy. Yes, maybe I brought you flowers and made meals for you, but if you must know, Barbara confronted me about the flowers and said I needed to stop cutting flowers from your father's garden or else she'd tell him and I'd be fired. Do you want that?"

Alice's heart squeezed. "No, but—"

"As for the meals, I made them when I was supposed to be working in the garden. There, again, I risked getting fired and I just can't do that anymore."

Alice nodded, brushing a tear from her cheek.

"I'm not trying to be hurtful, but you wanted to talk about this, so here's the truth. If you need someone to give you constant attention and lavish you with baubles, maybe you need to find another man."

"Jack, no!" She slammed her palms against the mirror.

The view in the vanity mirror swiveled as if Jack had dropped his hand mirror. All Alice could see was the library ceiling, but she heard him stomp out of the room and slam the door right on her heart.

"Jack?"

The mirror's image swirled into a rainbow of colors.

That Jack was just another Jack in her dream, but it was so damn hard to separate him from the real Jack. Right now she needed stay in this dream. She needed to learn how to have the confidence, courage, and charisma of a queen to prepare herself just in case Jack had any intention of breaking up with her the way he did just now. If that exchange was anything like what she could expect after waking up, she needed to first become that irresistible eight-horse woman.

The vanity mirror returned to normal. Alice eyed it and only saw herself. She thought of her original reason for taking on this journey, her wish for Jack to treat her the way he once did.

Alice whispered, "I miss you too, Jack."

18. A Devilish Egg

The ribs, the blood, and the skin are not enough.
A woman's heart must be properly packaged.

Square Six

A LICE picked up her courage, reminded herself that Jack hadn't actually broken up with her, and headed through a forest of sea-trees in the direction of the next square. She breathed in the fresh, salty air. It tasted like a fresh start. At a clearing, she spotted an egg perfectly perched on a red and orange wall. Sounds of women screaming came from the wall.

As she approached, however, the egg was hardly egg-shaped at all, but looked more like a young man in ivory clothes. The orange part of the wall, the lower half, seemed to be moving.

She stepped closer. The orange wall was actually a pack of naked women howling, pouncing, and pawing for the man who sat at the top. Alice plugged her ears from all the noise they made from their screams. This group of women acting so desperate for a man's attention looked ridiculous, and reminded her of a Beatles film she saw, "A Hard Day's Night."

A fresh, crisp, and musky scent she had never smelled before filled her lungs. It smelled amazing, like he was the earth, sea, and wind all at once, setting her on fire.

Alice peered at the top of the brick wall and caught her breath. She melted into a moistened well.

The man sitting there was the most handsome devil she'd ever seen. It wasn't his auburn hair or the almond-brown eyes. It wasn't the Roman nose or the hard jawline, nor was it the prominent cheekbones. It wasn't his ivory vest and thin, matching tie. So what was it? She couldn't put her finger on it, but that aspect of him that made him so sexy was on the tip of her tongue… and stewed at the tips of her nipples.

His gaze fell upon Alice. Her heart leapt. He spotted her. He scowled, straightened his ivory tie, tugged down his matching vest, and adjusted the cuffs of his button-up shirt.

He said something to Alice, but she couldn't hear it over the din of the women's shouts. She shook her head and shrugged to let him know, all while covering her ears over the din.

He rolled his eyes, held up a palm, and bellowed, "Stop!"

All the women fell silent.

"Sit," he commanded them.

They obeyed, dropping to the ground with frowns. They leaned against the wall facing Alice, none of them bothering with covering their breasts, or showing any sign of modesty.

This man's command over them made Alice shiver with excitement. She remembered that almost naughty game of Simon Says she'd once played with Troy as a girl. The power Troy had over her thrilled her in unexpected ways. Now, again, here was a man with power and confidence. Alice's nipples stood on end, aching to be touched.

"Who are you?" the man asked.

Alice stammered, "You're... you're gorgeous."

He let out an exasperated sigh. "Yes, I know. I use magic for that. I also know that my name is Roger Lodger, F.G. Now, what is yours?"

"Alice is my given name. What I mean is that my parents named me Alice and so I grew up that way and I never really liked it but I never officially changed it either and so I uh... I'm blabbering, aren't I?"

"Don't trouble yourself about it. It's the magic. Every woman responds that way." He scrutinized Alice. "Believe it or not, I used to be ignored. I recognize others who go through the pain I once experienced myself. Here's a poem you ought to hear about that." Roger cleared his throat, then recited the poem.

There was a gal who posed a pout
While sitting on a gate.
She wore a dress and heavy sigh
In such a sorry state.

And with her head upon her hand,
Her elbow on her thigh,
She didn't see the angels that were
Hovering nearby.

"What troubles you?" I asked the lass.
She lifted up her head.
"It's nothing you could help me with,"
The troubled maiden said.

She choked a sob and killed a cry.
I urged her on to speak.
"It's best you share your sorrows, dear,
To find the peace you seek."

She searched the ground for words to say,
Her sorrow to impart.
"I mated with a handsome man,
A gardener with a heart.

"He showed me all his love for days
He showed me every hour.
But now I'm ugly, that's the truth.
His love for me's gone sour."

Alice gulped. A shiver pierced down her back as Roger continued his poem.

> She did not let me meet her eye,
> Nor let her face be seen.
> "Whenever we're alone I think
> He'll treat me like a queen.
>
> "He used to bring me flowers, and he
> Used to bake me bread.
> But now I only see him when
> It's time to go to bed.
>
> "He stuffs himself inside of me,
> He acts as if he cares.
> But even then I feel alone."
> Her voice conveyed despair.
>
> The girl too shy at first to share
> About her living hell,
> She beat her chest and begged to die.
> The tears now finally fell.
>
> "Why?" She shouted to the heavens,
> Angels in the sky.
> "Why does he not love me now?
> Why?" She called out. "Why?"

Alice couldn't face Roger anymore. She dropped her eyes to the ground. Roger continued.

She did not realize how much
Her beauty, it could flower.
She did not know the joy she sought
Was all within her power.

I wished her well and journeyed on,
Ashamed I had not spoken.
I could have helped her mend her heart,
The one so clearly broken.

And now if e'er I see a girl
Who needs a better day,
I do not hesitate to voice
What she must hear one say.
For if I walk away from one
Who's in a sorry state,
I think of *her* who heaved a sigh,
The girl who leaned upon her thigh,
The girl who choked and killed her cry
To keep her cheeks still mostly dry,
The girl who would not meet my eye,
Who beat her heart and hoped to die,
The girl who shouted to the sky
Demanding for a reason why,
When all the while her joy stood by
Inside a knot *she could untie—*
The girl whose angels flew nearby
While sitting on a gate.

*****

ALICE'S heart wrenched. She bit her lip to fight back the sobs trembling in her throat.

"Alice, I have an offer for you. If you can answer a riddle, I'll use my magic to make you desirable by all men, including Jack."

"Yes, anything."

"Very well. You have three chances to get one right. Here's the first riddle. 'You've never met him, but follow his ways. You've never heard him, but do what he says. You played with him often with no chance of cheating, and now fantasize of him, with no interest of meeting. Who is he?' "

Alice worked it through.

Never met him, but follow his ways, like a politician or a celebrity, perhaps?

Never heard him suggested that if he was a celebrity, then he wasn't a singer or in the movies. A silent film, perhaps? Like Charlie Chaplin? But Alice didn't follow Charlie Chaplin's ways.

According to the riddle, she played with him and fantasized about him, but had no interest in meeting him?

Alice was stumped. It didn't matter. She had two more chances.

"I give up," Alice said.

"The correct answer is 'Simon.' "

Alice scowled. *Simon?*

Then it hit her. Of course the answer was Simon.

She had played Simon Says all the time, following his ways, and doing what he said. There was no chance of cheating in the game because anyone who didn't do the command would simply be cut from the game.

What about the fantasies? Alice shuddered. Yes, she had fantasies of playing Simon Says with Troy, but in a very adult fashion. How did this Roger fellow know about her fantasies?

Alice crossed her arms. "What's the second riddle?"

Roger nodded and spoke. "Her name is mixed of not one rodent but many, and a carpenter at a pole. She seeks out a tension from not many but one, a servant who could fill a hole. Who is she?"

Alice shuffled the words in her head. This one was harder than the first. Who was she?

Start with the name, she ordered herself. Many rodents? Rats, perhaps. Mice or squirrels were other possibilities. A carpenter at a pole? Like a telephone pole? Nothing came to mind for that one.

Alice worked over the rest of the riddle. Someone who wanted tension? Who would want tension? Maybe it wasn't a person. These riddles often personified objects. A bridge needed tension to stay up. And it might fill the gap between lands, acting as a servant for anyone who needed to cross. Rats, bridge, telephone pole...

Alice couldn't work it out. Was she overthinking it? The solution didn't come. She had one chance left.

"I give up," Alice said and shrugged.

He tsked. "The correct response is 'mice-elf.' "

Alice scowled. Mice was the word for many rodents, elf described a carpenter at the North Pole, but the rest? Who wanted tension from a servant who filled a hole?

Alice's gut sank. She muttered the words aloud. "Mice-elf. Myself. The answer is me."

Jack was the very man who filled her hole, both the physical hole of her desire and the emotional hole of her heart.

"I misunderstood. I thought you said 'a tension,' not 'attention.' "

Roger blinked and said, "Last chance, Alice. Here it is. 'She has a craft of weaving the proof of happy pups with glass and fragile will, and she keeps a baton without the black to smash against her skill. What does she have?' "

Alice flashed all the words through her head. She had to get this one right. Had to. If she got it right, Roger would use his magic to make her irresistible to Jack.

Weaving the proof of happy pups. The proof of happy pups could be tongues hanging out, wagging tails. Tails? Weaving tails? Yes. Weaving tales. The past two riddles were about her. This one must be about her, too. Weaving tales was her skill. What about the glass and fragile will? Nothing came to mind. She moved on, excited. She could get this one.

She keeps a baton without the black to smash against her skill? What kind of batons smashed?

Alice talked it out. "Canes, staffs, scepters. No, it's probably something specifically for smashing. Billie clubs, hammers, something without the black. A blackjack! So then..." Alice chilled as she realized the answer. She rubbed away the goosebumps on her arms.

Her craft, her skill, was the ability to weave tales. But "skill" was just another word for "art." Jack smashed her fragile "skill."

"Well?" Roger said. "What does she have?"

Alice answered with a small voice. "A broken art."

Roger peered gravely at Alice and nodded. "She does have that, doesn't she?"

Alice lowered her eyes.

The women were sneering at her, wearing twisted grins.

"Well done, Alice," Roger said and snapped his fingers. "What you seek is at that tree."

Alice turned to find the tree he indicated. Draped on its branches was a dazzling dandelion-colored gown and matching lingerie. At the base of the tree lay open-toe slippers, and other items too small to identify.

Alice dashed to the tree and took down the dress. Her chest bubbled with joy. She held it in front of her. It would look magnificent on her.

"Do you like it?" Roger asked. He was smiling

with lovely crooked teeth, the first time Alice had seen him smile.

"Very much," Alice beamed. At the foot of the tree lay a bottle of perfume, lipstick, and two jewelry boxes. She couldn't wait to see what precious items lay inside. Her eyes shifted to the lingerie, a lacy bra and a thong. Hmm.

"Something wrong?"

"No." Alice frowned. "It's just, the underwear doesn't look very comfortable."

He shook his head. "Do you wish to be comfortable or admired? Though having both is possible, I'm afraid in the world of clothing it's often one or the other." He adjusted his tie and scratched his neck. "I can assure you, the curse is not gender specific."

Alice smirked and nodded. She lay the dress, bra, and thong across one arm, and gathered the lipstick, perfume, jewelry boxes from the foot of the tree. "I'll be right back."

Behind the tree she changed into the lacy underwear. The lace of the bra lay across her nipples and Alice thought some chafing might occur. Still, she couldn't deny the seductive look of the see-through material. The thong slipped on well, but she'd have to get used to having fabric between her cheeks. The short-sleeved dress had a square neckline that came close to her nipples. So lovely. Alice smiled.

If Jack saw me now, he'd drool a pond.

On the ground rested the jewelry boxes. She wanted to save the best for last. For now, she picked up the lipstick. A fleeting thought of Lucy passed through her mind, but Alice chased it away. She painted her lips, popping them together to spread the coat. She then smelled the perfume. Mmm. Peaches. One whiff of this and Jack would want to eat her. Hell, any man would.

As Alice spritzed some of the perfume onto her neck and chest, she considered the musky scent she detected when first seeing Roger. Maybe that was his magic. His scent. The way his vest wrapped against his chest and the way his pants hugged his bulging parts probably also had something to do with it too.

Alice slipped her feet into the open-toed shoes. Her heart quivered when she saw the jewelry boxes at her feet. She picked up and opened the small one. Alice gasped. Golden earrings with tiny queen chess pieces dangled from them. Alice put them on wishing she had a mirror. The last box contained a golden necklace with a thin chain and an emblem of a crown. The crown had ruby jewels. So lovely!

Alice put on the necklace, flicking her hair out free over her shoulders, and remembered Queen Carol's riddle: *The ribs, the blood, and the skin are not enough. A woman's heart must be properly packaged.*

Alice twirled around and laughed, watching the skirt lift and flutter. Indeed, she was now properly packaged. She listened to the voices at her ears. The buzzing of the honey be's reminded her, "You will always be treasured. You will always be adored. You will always be cherished."

Alice felt her beauty inside and out.

She came out from behind the tree.

Roger smiled. "You look positively radiant."

The naked women glared at Alice, shooting jealous glances at her. She could get used to that.

Roger said, "The only thing left for you to do is to choose to be a beauty queen. You now have the ability to shine."

Alice took a deep breath and smiled.

Roger muttered, "In truth, you always had the ability to shine, I just helped you find your glow."

Alice scowled. She knew what he meant. In the story of the eight-horse woman, Nathaniel's love for Solette helped Solette realize how beautiful she was. Here, the clothes and jewelry Alice wore acted like Nathaniel's love, making it easier for Alice to believe in her own beauty.

Glancing down, she admired how well her shape filled out the dress. Her heart warmed.

Roger said, "Seeing you reminds me of the first time I felt handsome."

So he knows what I'm feeling right now. "Roger, when you told me your name, you said some letters after your name."

He smiled. "Yes. Roger Lodger F.G."

"What do those letters stand for?"

"Fairy Godfather," he said. Were his eyes welling with tears? "It is time for you to journey to the next square."

"Of course," Alice curtsied. "I bid you farewell, my great Fairy Godfather."

"Yeah, yeah. Get out of here before I cry." He addressed the women at his feet. "Ladies, you may continue."

The women pounced to their feet and howled for his attention, some struggling to climb the wall.

Alice hitched up her skirt and hustled into the nearby forest wishing she had four hands, two to hold up her dress and two to plug her ears from the women's screams.

19. The Leo and the Uniquus

A horse and a lion will just never heed
How the best resolution is what they both need.

To Square Seven

AS SOON as Alice entered the forest to reach the next square, she shivered. A cold chill passed through her. Was that a premonition of something bad to come?

Alice did indeed worry about having another fight with Jack once she woke up. Arguing with him hurt so much. She had relied on his love so much. He made her feel comfortable and stable. When he was upset it felt like the floor fell out from underneath her. At least now she was still in a dream, safe from fighting Jack.

So what was that cold chill? Would something bad happen in the dream? She shivered again. The chill returned with a harsher bite. Nope, not a premonition, just cold.

Alice grimaced and rubbed her bare arms as she ventured deeper into the woods. She liked the cold, but sometimes the chill could make concentrating quite tiresome in a dream.

The trees were labeled with signs. At first, Alice thought they were directions, but taking a closer look showed the signs to be of no help at all.

Some trees read, "Right." Others read, "Wrong." Some said, "Correct," and others said, "Incorrect." Some trees were marked, "Proper" and others were marked, "Improper." One tree, which had the tips of its branches cut off, bore the sign, "Kosher."

Ridiculous. What made a tree right or wrong? Proper or improper?

A wind whipped through. Alice shivered from the biting cold. On one tree, a heavy coat hung on a branch.

Good. That would help her out. She lifted the black, wool coat off the branch and slipped it on. It felt so soft, the inner lining must have been made of silk. The thick soft material was just what she needed.

Alice trudged deeper into the woods. A figure

flitted across her path, and forged through the trees ahead of her.

What was that? She couldn't tell if it was man or beast.

She peered into the distance, and gasped. It was some kind of magnificent horse. The creature galloped between the trees with grace and ease, then switched to a trot. Alice gasped again when she saw its face—a man's face. Was it a centaur? The horse's neck was, instead, the torso of a well-built man, complete with muscular arms and hands. Couldn't be a centaur. A centaur didn't have a horn on its forehead like this one had. And though the horn resembled one belonging to a unicorn, he couldn't be a unicorn. Unicorns didn't look like men.

Alice needed to get to the coronation, but there was no risk of waking up. Neither the black knight nor Jack was anywhere nearby. Curiosity caught the better of Alice and she scurried after the creature. The beast entered a clearing. On its four horse legs, it elegantly stepped up to an orange pond and bent at the waist. It cupped a bit of the orange water in its hands and drank.

Lord, the creature was beautiful. She tiptoed closer for a better look. He had a lock of straw blond hair hanging over his royal blue eyes. His naked chest and arms bore modest muscles. The rest of his body from his waist to his wispy tail resembled that of an ivory horse.

An armadillo ambled into the clearing and tumbled over a rock, spilling itself into the pond.

The centaur-looking creature splashed into the orange water and recovered the armadillo, the reptile's body in his arms.

He carried the armadillo to the grassy earth, wiping dry its wet shell. "There you are. Safe and dry."

The creature said something else Alice couldn't hear, so she edged into the grassy clearing.

The man-beast raised his head and twitched his nose. He flexed his leg muscles and galloped across the clearing, into the woods, and out of sight.

Alice sighed with disappointment. That was one stunning beauty.

A wisp of wind fluttered behind her. Alice gasped and turned around. A glimpse of hooves disappeared into the woods.

Then two arms grabbed her from behind. A snort of breath huffed at her neck.

Alice peered behind her. It was the same man from the pond, but now he had the body of a regular man.

And he was naked.

The man pressed his body behind her and inhaled at her neck. "I thought I smelled peaches. I was right." He squeezed her closer to him. "Did you steal that perfume from Roger? Are you a thief, you black pawn?"

Alice trembled at being trapped in this man's arms. Black pawn? Why did he think she was a black pawn? A more pressing question begged to be asked.

"What are you going to do to me?"

He smelled her scent again and let out a sigh of delight. "I will do as the white queen expects. I will capture the black pieces in play. You, my delicious lady, will be my captive. I claim you. You are mine."

Alice had to smile at what that might be like. This dream was getting better and better. Her ring buzzed at her finger. Were its vibrations a warning or an approval?

"Once you claim me," she said, "what will you do to me?"

"Perhaps the queen will let me keep you, and I'll take you to my stables." His hands wandered across her belly, edging closer to her covered breasts. "Have you ever slept in hay before?"

"No," Alice breathed. She placed her hands on his arms to help guide his caresses up her chest.

He inhaled her scent again. "On especially cold nights, you will keep me warm and let me fill you with my seed."

Being taken by such a man in hay? That sounded magnificent. But he'd have to hurry, or else she'd wake up and lose the chance of enjoying him.

Alice laced her fingers in his, steering him over her coat to her breasts. "I thought you were part horse."

"Shapeshifter." He squeezed her breasts.

Lord, that was wonderful. Alice moaned.

"I'm a horned centaur when I need to move, and on occasion, I am a man when I need to satisfy my desires."

She felt him harden behind her. She arched her back to nuzzle against his hands and to stiffen him further. Did he still have...?

Alice reached up behind her to his forehead. Yes. He still had a horn.

With one hand, he lifted her coat and dress, and nudged his cock against her. Alice pulled aside her thong and guided him into her.

He slammed in. She cried out at the pleasure he pushed into her.

He growled, "Let's get this coat off you." He ripped the coat off her shoulders, then let go of her and backed away. "Heavens, what have I done?"

Why did he stop? Alice turned to see what was wrong, the coat dangling off her shoulders.

He stammered. "You're not a black pawn. You're on my side, on the path to queenhood." He sank to his knees. "My lady, I beg your forgiveness."

Alice squirmed uncomfortable at the situation. "Why are you apologizing?"

"My lady, if I had known you were the very one I should be helping on the path to coronation, I would not have attacked you so brutally as I did."

"Well," Alice muttered, "it wasn't that brutal."

"Please forgive me, my lady. How can I make it

up to you."

All right. I can play that game.

"If you wish to be forgiven, come kiss me."

The one-horned man bowed. "As you wish, my lady."

He approached her, but Alice thought of Jack and couldn't help feeling guilty. The man held her arms and leaned in for the kiss.

"Wait," she said, holding her hand up to stop him.

A voice growled behind her, "What's going on, Uniquus?"

A broad-shouldered man with a mane of long, golden hair stood beside a tree wearing only a loincloth.

Alice's centaur, the man whose name apparently was Uniquus, huffed back, "Leave us, Leo."

"I will not." Leo padded closer. "Too often you've mistaken our own players as the enemy. That cannot happen again."

Uniquus let go of Alice's arms. "I apologize, my lady. This brute knows not what he is saying."

Leo roared, "You're the one who sacrifices our allies from the game and you call me a brute? I'll show you what a brute can do."

Leo's mouth and nose cracked into a growing protrusion, forming a snout.

Alice gasped. *What's going on?*

Uniquus shouted a primal scream of challenge.

His back oozed out a pair of hind legs, extending into a thick, ivory torso of a horse.

Leo dropped onto all fours, his hands and feet filling out into giant paws.

Alice staggered back. Leo bounded toward Uniquus across the grassy field. Uniquus charged into Leo. They collided and rolled onto the dirt, clawing, stamping, biting, chomping.

Someone tapped Alice on the shoulder.

Alice spun and welcomed the friendly face. "Hyde!"

He smiled. "How are you enjoying yourself, Alice? Have you learned much?"

Alice pointed to the angry brawl between Leo and Uniquus, snorting and growling as they tumbled in the grass. "Shouldn't we stop them?"

Hyde turned to watch the fight. He shrugged, "They'll be fine. They fight all the time."

"Really?" Alice looked carefully. It's true that neither actually bled from the chomping and biting, pawing and wrestling.

"Which one do you think is right?" Hyde asked. "Uniquus or Leo?"

"Which one is right?" Alice scratched her head. "I hardly think either one is right or wrong. Like the trees."

Hyde laughed. "Precisely. Isn't it ridiculous how they're on the same side and yet they fight all the time?"

Alice bit back a laugh, catching herself from pointing out how Hyde and Jackyll also fought all the time. She imagined such fights were just like the quarrels of lovers.

Alice thought of Jack, and their own lover's quarrel in the early morning. Could that have been Queen Carol's lesson?

A horse and a lion will just never heed
How the best resolution is what they both need.

It dawned on Alice. The queen wasn't saying that Leo and Uniquus both need a best resolution, she was saying that to resolve their fights they should focus on what they both needed.

Leo and Uniquus both wanted the same thing, to win the chess game for their queen. So why did they fight?

Alice shivered, in realization, not for the cold. In the case of her and Jack, they both wanted a good relationship, so why did they fight?

From now on, she needed to become aware of every moment she had the desire to express a complaint against Jack. She had to recognize those moments and instead of seeking to help herself, she needed to ask herself, "How will this help our relationship?"

Jack and I both want to be in a good relationship. Why fight if we both want the same thing?

Alice shivered again. Hyde stepped behind her and raised her coat back over her shoulders. "You look as though you're ready to move on."

Alice watched Leo and Uniquus tumble in the grass without really seeing them. She nodded to Hyde.

"Come." He took her hand. "I have a horse nearby we can ride. I'll escort you to the coronation."

Alice held Hyde's warm hand, walking in a daze.

20. The Black Knight

I fear you'll not know the answer to this one.
When the black knight forces you into decision,
The sad truth of it all is, to follow your lie,
You must let the secret of your little deaths die.

<u>Square Seven</u>

ALICE rode sidesaddle on the horse as Hyde walked in front, holding on to the horse's reins, leading the horse through the woods. The air felt thicker now and warm. Her clothes clung to her skin through her sweat. She slipped off the coat and hung it on a passing branch. Hyde glanced back at her. She smiled. The forest was full of looking-glass leaves reflecting her green surroundings in a shimmering mosaic.

So Jack and I don't need to fight. We both want a

good relationship. We both want to love each other properly.

Alice twirled a lock of her hair.

Figuring out how to love each other properly sure would be easier if Alice knew why Jack loved her.

Hyde glanced back again. Why was he always looking back at her?

"What's wrong?" Alice asked. "Do I have something between my teeth?" She licked her teeth to make sure nothing was there.

"No, no," Hyde laughed. "You're just stunning. Much more beautiful than when Jackyll and I first met you."

Alice caught herself from replying. She was about to say, I know. For the first time, she felt her beauty was a fact. To deny it would be lying.

Time to practice modesty. "It's the dress and jewelry. They're what make me look so pretty."

Hyde chuckled, leading the horse. "Your dress and jewelry? You might want to take a closer look at what you're wearing."

Alice looked down at her dress. It didn't drape around her at all. In fact, the dress looked painted on, as did the necklace on her chest.

Alice held onto the saddle with one hand and with the other hand touched what she thought was fabric on her breasts. It wasn't fabric, she was naked. Then the painted look vanished to reveal her true skin shade. How odd.

"What's going on?"

"You're accepting your outer beauty," Hyde said. "You now have the eyes to see how gorgeous you are." He stopped and the horse stopped too. "Climb down for a moment." Grabbing her at her hips, he hoisted her off the horse and onto the ground. He rummaged through a saddlebag and pulled out a hand mirror. "Here we go. Take a closer look at yourself with your new eyes."

Hyde held up the mirror. Alice traced her thin eyebrows, seeing how they framed the top of her eyes. She slid her fingers down the bridge of her small nose and down to her lips, the very lips Jack had kissed with his own. She touched the slight dimple in her chin, the one she had once thought was unfeminine but now looked beautiful, as if the dimple were a medal of her courage and boldness.

Hyde lowered the mirror to her neck. "Explore further. See your beauty."

She glided her hands down her neck, so sensual, so easy to adore. She touched her bare shoulders, thinking of how alluring they could be when peeking out from a dress. She cupped her breasts feeling the satisfying weight of men's lust filling her hands. She traced her nipples, so pink that their very color exuded her femininity. She reached down her belly, and with her fingertips, followed the slight fold where the belly met her waist. What she once considered fat now looked desirable, a smile at her torso, and it was hers. This was who she was.

Hyde said, "Turn around."

She obeyed. Hyde held the mirror low and she could see her full bottom in the reflection. The curves invited, and for the first time she understood why Jack enjoyed touching her there so much.

Alice took it all in. She was beautiful. To wear clothes now seemed a shame. Like covering up a masterpiece. Alice wanted to remain naked for everyone, herself included, to appreciate her beauty.

Hyde placed a hand on her shoulder and turned her to face him. He caressed her cheek and kissed her. "Come. The coronation is in ten minutes."

A warm wind blew against her chest. Lavender wafted in the air. She curled her toes in the moist grass. "Why don't you ride the horse? I'd like to walk and feel the ground."

"As you wish." Hyde climbed upon the saddle and clicked his tongue, urging the horse forward.

Alice strode beside him, holding the horse's reins. The honey be's buzzed around her whispering, "You will always be treasured. You will always be desired. You will always be craved."

She glanced up at Hyde when she felt his eyes on her. Hyde gazed fondly at her. She breathed in the adoration, understanding why he couldn't keep his eyes off her. Her body conveyed the beauty of who she was inside.

Suddenly a branch snapped into Alice's face so

hard she staggered backwards and cried out in surprise.

"Alice!" Hyde leaned down from the horse and reached out for her. "Are you alright?"

That was odd. She didn't feel any pain or sting. The branch hit her hard enough to push her back. Shouldn't she have felt it?

"Alice?"

"I'm fine." Alice touched her face searching for a cut. "What I don't understand is why it didn't hurt."

"Oh, dear." Hyde grimaced. "I hope it's not what I think it is. Come here."

Alice stepped closer to the side of the horse. Hyde reached down, and with his hands under her armpits, he heaved her up and lay her across his lap face down. "Tell me how this feels."

He spanked her. At least, that's what it sounded like to Alice. She didn't feel anything, and she couldn't see what his hand was slapping, but by the thwacking sounds and the way her body jilted forward on his lap with each thwack, he must have been spanking her.

He kept on whacking her. "What do you feel?"

"Not a thing," Alice grunted, grabbing on to the saddlebag for balance.

He rubbed her bottom. "And now?"

Whoa! There it was. A prickling memory of his slaps smoothed out by his delicious caresses.

Alice enjoyed his touch. "I can feel your hand now."

Hyde lifted her up. "Sit facing me."

She opened her legs and straddled Hyde's lap, intrigued by what this position might lead to.

He said, "I'm very sorry."

"For what?"

"For this." He slapped her across the face. "Did you feel that?"

Alice was stunned, but realized why he had slapped her. "I didn't feel it at all."

Hyde gently kissed her cheek. Her cheek tingled under his lips. He kissed other parts of her face, her neck, and her breasts.

She leaned back to help him fill his mouth with her. Her nipples hardened at the touch of his lips. So good.

He slapped her face again. He peered at her with an inquisitive expression.

"Nothing," Alice said. "I felt no pain at all."

He frowned and nodded. "It's just as I feared. Your body is in mourning."

"How so?"

"You've chosen to be a queen, Alice. A queen is never spanked nor slapped."

Alice scowled. "So I can't feel rough treatment?"

Hyde shrugged. "A part of you can, but that part of you is not with you now."

Over her shoulder, she saw the one she feared. The black knight. He approached in full armor on a horse, his horse clopping in precise movements. The knight wore a helmet, obscuring his face. He alighted his horse.

"I've come to take her back." The black knight's voice was of a woman, not of a man. Here was the one who could wake Alice up. Why did she want to take Alice? And to where? Back to the real world?

Hyde steered his horse to the side of the path and stopped. "You cannot. She has chosen to be queen."

The knight placed a hand on her sword's hilt. "Her choice is flawed. Even you know that."

"True, but her choice is her own to make. No one else's."

"Then to support her decision, you must fight for her. Show her what her choice truly means." The black knight drew her sword.

"As you wish." He picked Alice up off his lap.

"Wait." Alice gripped Hyde's arms as he set her down on the ground. "I thought you said we only have a few minutes before the coronation."

Hyde unsheathed his sword and muttered, "We have time for her. This knight deserves our attention."

Alice's ring vibrated on her finger. She scowled. "What do you mean?"

The black knight charged at Hyde. Hyde raised his sword and blocked the black knight's attack. He shoved the knight against a tree.

Alice felt an invisible force push her back against another tree. What was that force?

Hyde slammed the knight's sword-wielding hand against the tree, forcing the knight to drop her sword.

Alice's wrist pierced with pain. "Ow!"

Hyde called out to Alice, "Remember how I said the part of you that can feel rough treatment isn't with you anymore?"

Alice bit her lip at the pain in her wrist and wriggled against the invisible force pushing her against the tree. "Yes."

"Here she is. Here's that part of you." Hyde yanked off the knight's helmet.

It was the sneering Alice, the one from the mirror that morning in Jack's room.

Alice gasped at the knight's true identity. "You!"

The knight put her armored arms around Hyde's shoulders. "Take me, Hyde. Show her how much she doesn't want to be queen."

Hyde called out to Alice, "She's right. I need to show you what you're denying yourself."

Hyde let his sword drop to the ground, reached at his belt and retrieved a dagger. The knight smiled and raised her arms above her head against the tree. Hyde sliced through the straps of her breastplate and the armor landed on the ground with a clang. He cut through the ties of her gauntlets and thigh armor.

All Alice could feel was the insistent shoving against the tree from the invisible force that, she now understood, was Hyde shoving himself against the knight.

Underneath the knight's thigh-high chainmail, she was naked.

Hyde kicked aside the armor on the ground, the pieces clattered out of the way.

He clamped his hands on the knight's breasts, pressing them and squeezing them through the chainmail.

The knight didn't seem to respond, but Alice felt her own nipples being pinched by invisible chainmail. Alice moaned at the arousal that spiked through her body. Why did it feel good?

Hyde clenched the knight's nipples between his thumbs and forefingers.

The ring on Alice's finger buzzed aggressively. Alice cupped her breasts, working to rub away the pain at her tips, but not entirely wanting to rid herself of the stimulation. She touched her vibrating ring to her nipple. Her nipples hardened. Did the knight feel the same thing? She didn't seem to be affected at all by Hyde's sadistic hands.

Am I the only one who feels what Hyde is doing?

Before Alice could dwell too long on that, Hyde nudged the knight's legs apart and with a cupped hand, slapped a handful of chainmail against her pussy.

Alice yelped. She rubbed her clit to ease the sharp pain. It tingled from the slap. Alice shivered wondering why she was so wet.

The knight laughed at Alice.

I suppose I am a sight to behold, rubbing myself in all the intimate spots.

Then Alice felt something working inside her, prickling and tickling her delicate folds along the way. What in heaven's name?

From what Alice could see, Hyde was stuffing the knight with chainmail.

Alice's blood pounded through her body as she stifled the delicious pinching and prickling with her own vigorous fingers, vibrating her bud, penetrating and stirring inside her core.

She clenched around her fingers. Lord, it felt so good.

The knight laughed hysterically. That woman probably didn't feel anything of what Hyde did to her.

Hyde turned the knight so she faced the tree.

Alice felt shoved around, that invisible force mashing her body against her own tree. She still had a clear view of what Hyde was set out to do. Watching him tug off his belt set Alice dripping with anticipation.

Am I excited at the idea of seeing Hyde smack the smile off the knight's face? Or am I actually looking forward to getting belted?

Thwack!

Alice cried out. A rush of excitement passed through her, like she had fallen off a cliff but knew she would be caught.

Thwack!

Alice yelped. Despite the pink stripes on the knight's bottom, the woman kept laughing. Alice peeked behind her and noticed no marks down there.

So I feel the pain, but my body remains unharmed.

Thwack!

Alice shouted out a cry of pleasure. This was wrong. She shouldn't be enjoying this. No one is supposed to enjoy a thrashing. Memories of actually getting pleasure from being punished as a girl bubbled to the surface. At the time, she was too young to pin anything sexual to delighting in the punishment, so she merely dismissed it.

Thwack!

"Ow!" Alice rubbed herself between her legs. Now there was no reason to deny it. Alice felt sexual pleasure from the belting, even though she knew it was wrong. A fist of guilt clenched inside her gut.

Thwack!

Alice moaned. Her guilty pleasure dripped all over her fingers.

Hyde stood back from the knight, the belt in his hand poised to strike again. "Do you wish me to continue? Or do you wish to be treated like a queen?"

Alice stood upright and rubbed her bottom. The delicious tingling made her feel alive, as though she had been dead inside and needed to wake up.

But such things were perverted. Only deviants

and degenerates enjoyed being abused. And what would Jack think? He'd drop her in an instant if he thought she enjoyed getting belted. Alice knew what the right choice was.

"I choose to be treated like a queen."

"Then take off your ring and make the decision final."

"My ring?"

"Yes. The one Jack gave you at the fair."

"But—" Alice said, twirling the buzzing ring around her finger, "how can I let go of one of my favorite memories of Jack?"

"Memories aren't real. Only the present is real. The choices you make will determine every present moment for the rest of your life. Do you wish to be treated like a queen?"

"Yes, I do." With one hand, she worked at rubbing away the sting on her bottom. "But what does wearing the ring have to do with it?"

"It's the only way."

The knight shook her head, "Don't do it, Alice. The ring will guide you. You must keep it on."

Hyde sighed, pulled out a watch on a chain, then tucked it away. "You have less than two minutes to get to the coronation, if that's what you want. You've made your choice, now let that choice define the rest of your life."

"No, Alice." The knight looked sincere. "Don't do it. Let me wake you up."

Alice snorted at the woman, "I'm supposed to trust you?" The woman had spent most of her time laughing at Alice, making fun of her. Hyde was right. There wasn't much time left. After all, the whole thing was just a dream. She'd wake up with the ring still on her finger.

Alice worked the ring off. As soon as the ring came off, the knight cried out and hissed, clutching the pink stripes on her bottom.

Alice realized all her own stinging spikes of pain disappeared. They must have transferred to the knight. That was why the knight was so insistent on making sure Alice didn't take off the ring. The woman didn't want to feel the pain.

Hyde sheathed his dagger and sword, and mounted his horse.

The woman licked her palm and rubbed at the belt marks on her bottom, hissing at the pain.

Hyde motioned with his hand to her. "Come. Let's get you to the coronation."

Alice glanced around for a spot to set the ring down. She squatted at the base of the tree and gently placed the ring there.

Hyde heaved Alice up onto the horse as she was before, facing him with her legs apart.

The knight leaned against a tree, squeezing her breasts as if trying to soothe them from the sting Alice got to know and enjoy firsthand.

As the horse ambled away, Alice remembered

Queen Carol's words for this square.

> *I fear you'll not know the answer to this one.*
> *When the black knight forces you into decision,*
> *The sad truth of it all is, to follow your lie,*
> *You must let the secret of your little deaths die.*

Alice leaned against Hyde's chest.

To follow my lie I had to let my little deaths die?
What little deaths?

She thought of how "little death," or "*petit mort*" was the French term for orgasm. Was there a chance that she could no longer have orgasms?

"Is something troubling you?" Hyde's deep voice resounded against her cheek.

Alice smiled and let the riddle escape her. "It's nothing."

21. To the Coronation

You want to unlock the why of your lover.
The reason he loves you, you wish to discover.
On this piercing journey to your coronation,
The answer you'll learn before the destination.

<u>To Square Eight</u>

S EATED backwards on the horse, as naked as Lady Godiva, Alice leaned against Hyde's chest and arched her back. The horn of the saddle rubbed against her sweet spot. She squirmed and licked her lips. The air smelled of cinnamon.

They'd left the black knight so the knight was no threat to waking up Alice, but Hyde was right here.

According to Queen Carol, if Jack became upset—and Alice supposed that applied to every version of Jack in this wonderland—then Alice risked waking up before reaching the coronation.

Alice had no intention of upsetting Hyde. Though the top priority was getting to the coronation, she still needed delicious release. The climax she so desired shouldn't cause Hyde any stress.

"Hyde, how much time do we have?"

He checked his watch. "Humph. That's odd." He shook his watch by his ear.

Alice leaned back to see Hyde better. "What is it?"

"You still believe that you're dreaming, right?"

"Yes."

"Well, either you're dead, or my watch stopped." He shook it and checked again, frowning.

Alice shivered. That would be a twist. If she were dead then she'd be stuck in this wonderland forever. Alice dismissed the idea.

Something jingled. Hyde pulled out another watch from his coat.

Alice scowled. "You have two watches?"

"No, this one's Jackyll's. I took it when he wasn't looking."

"How come?"

"I bet him fifty pence that he'd lose his watch, and I don't like to lose." Hyde scrutinized the watch then snapped it closed and tucked it away in a vest pocket. "Good news. You're not dead."

"That's a relief."

"Even better news. We have fifteen minutes to get to the coronation, not two."

Alice warmed and traced a line down Hyde's chest. "I was just thinking."

"Yes?"

"I'll soon have my coronation, end my journey, and probably wake up into the real world."

Hyde nodded.

Alice ground her hips gently along the horn of the saddle and blushed. "So I'd love to have you take me. Rough. You know, as a sort of last hurrah."

"I can't do that."

She jolted back. "I don't understand. You did it to the knight." Her heart chilled. "I'm not good enough? Is that it?"

Hyde shook his head. "I'm the hidden side of Jack. The side you don't see and, as a queen, you will never see."

"What?" Alice huffed.

He was spouting nonsense. Maybe it was time to play by his rules.

She adjusted his collar and patted his chest. "I'm not queen, yet." She smiled coyly. "Isn't there still time?"

"No." Hyde focused past her to the path ahead. "You've already made your choice. You've removed your ring."

Alice slumped. Hyde made no sense. What did being a queen have to do with seeing different sides of Jack? Alice took in a deep breath of the cinnamon air and sighed out her disappointment. Even in her dream, she couldn't get him to treat her the way she wanted to be treated. Maybe once she was queen she could demand that he service her.

A breeze passed between them, the brief chill putting her bare nipples to attention. The horse ambled, cracking the cinnamon sticks on the path. Hyde kept glancing at her. Was that pity in his eyes?

After a moment, he cleared his throat and spoke. "Has anyone sung to you the song of what your coronation will be like and what your duties shall be?"

"No." Alice shrugged, like she even cared.

Hyde said nothing for a while, and then sang in a deep voice:

The queen-to-be shall be cleansed of every bit of her past.

He held her head to his chest. His words vibrated through her body.

Her outer skin is where they'll start first and her inner skin shall be the last.

He rubbed her mound, and then sunk a finger inside. Alice moaned.

The queen-to-be shall be placed on a throne.

He removed his finger, yanked her hips close to his, and ground his crotch against hers. She opened up to him, feeling his lust for her thick against his trousers. She had to remind herself that somewhere Jackyll felt her rubbing against him. The stiffness she felt between her thighs must have been Jackyll pumping himself to get Hyde hard. Good boy.

She'll be crowned and cloaked with a royal tone.

With desperate breaths, Alice tugged open his trousers and found Hyde's cock. He grabbed her fleshy rear in both hands and heaved her closer. He rubbed against her open folds.

The queen-to-be shall be never ignored.

Hyde's breaths became heavy. He held Alice so close, her nipples rubbed against his chest. She hung on to his torso and tightened her fists around his shirt.

A crown at her mind, a scepter in her core.

He dropped her onto him, stretching her, impaling her with the attention she desired. She moaned as she adjusted to his length.

Hyde clicked at the horse.

Alice gasped. The horse switched to a trot, pummeling her on Hyde's cock. She gripped him, riding him through the woods. Pops and sparks kicked through her chest. Her nipples sought relief as they rubbed against him.

Up and down, she bobbed upon him. Each time it felt like he had pounded further into her, lancing deeper inside. Her toes curled. She bit into his shoulder, doing so stifled the cry of orgasm that shuddered through her.

Hyde roared. Alice felt him splash spurt after spurt inside her.

Her legs trembled finding little to cling to even while passing through the gate of her climax, Hyde's softening cock continued penetrating her at the horse's trot. Alice's peak continued its course, rippling across her skin. She shook and squeezed her eyes shut.

Hyde commanded, "Whoa."

The horse stopped. Hyde remained inside of her.

Alice clenched her breasts, squeezing out the final tingling of her nipples. She cupped her clit. With gentle strokes, she mixed the last drops of her satiated desire along with Hyde's white pleasure dripping out from her.

Hyde eased her off of him and held her close.

Alice lay her head on his shoulder and sighed, boneless and content. "I loved that song."

"Mm. Yes." Hyde caressed her back. "It is a wonderful song. You should take pride in it. After all, you wrote it."

Alice laughed. "No, I didn't."

"Yes, you did." He stroked her hair. "This is your dream, remember? Everything that happens here is your creation."

Alice chuckled. He was just being his silly self. She played along. "Didn't you say that this was Jack's dream? And that if he woke up we'd all disappear?"

"Semantics. The point is, this is your creation. Your world. And that song I sang was written by you."

Alice frowned. "I don't remember writing it."

"You wrote it as I sang it. Every poem, every song, every square, every character here, even myself, we are all your creation." He pulled back and peered into Alice's eyes. "You have an amazing gift, Alice. Be proud of it. It's why Jack loves you so much."

Alice considered Jack. He had never told her why he loved her, just that he did. The why of his love for her escaped her. Alice didn't realize just how much that information meant to her until now. Knowing why Jack loved her filled a hole in her heart she didn't even know was there. What had Queen Carol said?

> *You want to unlock the why of your lover.*
> *The reason he loves you, you wish to discover.*
> *On this piercing journey to your coronation,*
> *The answer you'll learn before the destination.*

Alice dwelled on the new insight.

I am creative, and Jack loves me for it.

It didn't sit right with Alice. There were all sorts of artists, musicians, and authors that Alice loved. It didn't mean she wanted to marry any of them.

Hyde scrutinized her with concern. "What's wrong, Alice?"

She embraced Hyde. She held him tight, needing to feel him there with her.

"Nothing at all," she said.

Hyde clicked, urging the horse forward. They continued at a slow amble through the woods to reach the final square, a vast castle in the distance.

22. The Three Maidens and the Coronation

If you wish to be seen, how much will you reveal
Before your desire for privacy hides you again?

<u>Square Eight</u>

NAKED, Alice was coaxed by three maidservants wearing Renaissance aprons and bonnets into a dark hall of the castle. Even the stone walls harkened to days of the Renaissance or earlier, as though she were pulled back in time.

"Hurry, my lady." One of the women rushed her, grabbing her by the arm.

Hyde had brought Alice on his horse to the castle

and told the maidens to get her prepared for the coronation.

Now they urged her along with painful tugs to her arm as though their very lives depended upon getting her ready.

The torches' flickering lights caused shadows to dance along the hallway walls. The air smelled musty, as the traditions of centuries floated on the dust motes.

The three maidens escorted her through a tall doorway into a hot, brightly lit chamber. The moist heat felt good against her naked skin, but Alice had to squint against the too bright light.

The door shut with a whoosh behind her. Her eyes adjusted to the light. The three maidens rushed her to a modest wooden chair at the center of the chamber. Alice gasped. The walls were mirrors. She had never seen a mirror take up an entire wall, much less all four walls.

One of the maidens, an elderly woman with salt and pepper hair, wore a constant scowl and addressed the youngest servant. "Come help me move the washing basin."

"Of course, Mistress Ice." The young maiden's eyes remained wide open, as if she were afraid of disappointing Mistress Ice. Perhaps she had never faced such urgency before.

The two maidens moved to the corner of the room where a metal washbasin lay beside a table of skincare bottles, sponges, and makeup.

The third maiden, a plump and buxom lady who smiled with calm reassurance, caressed Alice's cheek. "You are so lovely. Don't you worry about a thing. We'll have you ready for the coronation in no time." Alice admired how this maiden's bust was so full it seemed ready to spill out of her dress at any laugh.

Alice squinted against the hot, piercing lights. "Why is it so bright in here?"

The buxom maiden chuckled. "That would be the lumen. See the gargoyle-type statues along the edges where the ceiling meets the walls?"

Glancing up, Alice eyed the many sculpted busts of men crafted along the ceiling's edges. All of them had their eyes on her, but looked indifferent and unaware of her presence. All of them had their mouths open and light spilled strong from their open jaws.

Alice sighed, her muscles relaxing, and let the light sink into her skin. The sculptures were like an audience staring at her naked form, and at the same time their soulless, vacant gazes gave her a sense of privacy.

Alice said under her breath, "Like being in a museum. A very calming effect."

"The lumen help us see our work," the cheerful woman said, "though it can get hot in here sometimes."

The one named Mistress Ice and the young

maiden lugged the washbasin beside Alice. Peering inside, Alice noticed it was full of white liquid. Why did the basin contain milk?

Then Alice remembered the storm of milk. If milk replaced the water of this world, then the milk in a washing basin was no longer outrageous.

Mistress Ice peered at Alice, then addressed the cowering maiden. "Let's start with the hair, La."

"Yes, miss." La cupped some milk in her hands, moved behind Alice, and poured it upon her head.

Alice felt the refreshing, cool milk seep onto her scalp. It smelled like peppermint. La ran her fingers through Alice's hair, then returned to the basin for another handful of milk.

As young La dampened Alice's hair, Mistress Ice said to the cheerful maiden. "Fetch some sponges, Lacie. And the rosemary essence."

Alice's new friend Lacie squeezed Alice's arm and smiled. "I'll be right back."

Alice closed her eyes. La's fingers felt good weaving through her hair.

When Alice opened her eyes, buxom Lacie had returned and handed a small, amber bottle to La. Lacie carried two sponges. She dipped them in the basin of milk and gave one to Mistress Ice. Lacie and Mistress Ice stood at either side of Alice, squeezed the cool peppermint milk onto her shoulders, and then rubbed it into her skin.

Alice welcomed the refreshing cool down in this

hot room full of mirrors. The milk dribbled down her chest and back, the scent of peppermint wafting in the air.

But there was another scent. Alice sniffed. Rosemary. By the way La worked her fingers through Alice's hair, La must have been cleansing her hair with the rosemary essence.

"Lather it up well and deep, La," Ice said. "She needs to smell completely relaxed."

Alice smiled.

"Yes, miss," La said and massaged Alice's scalp.

Alice moaned at the wonderfulness of La's skillful fingers touching all the right places on her head. She slid deeper into the chair. The rosemary essence bubbled. It had to be working as a kind of shampoo.

Mistress Ice and Lacie rubbed the peppermint milk with deep pressure into her shoulders.

Mmm, that felt good. Alice dropped her head forward and let her tension melt. Did the light go dim for a moment?

Alice looked up but there was no change in the bright beams coming from the statues' mouths. She gazed at the wall mirror in front of her. Something was wrong. What was it?

Alice sat up and squinted. The front mirror reflected the mirror behind her creating an infinite hallway of the likeness of Lacie, La, and Ice. But the reflections of the chair revealed the chair to be empty.

Alice frantically touched her smooth face, her

soapy hair, her warm chest. Was she even really there? She felt like she was in the room.

Young La asked, "Is something the matter, my lady?"

"Where's my reflection?" Alice checked her hands. She could see them, but not in the mirror. This was like being on the train again, completely invisible.

Lacie laughed. "Oh, my lady. You are much too unique to have a reflection."

What?

Mistress Ice peered into Alice's eyes. "There is only one of you, Alice. Now this is no time to wonder how good you look. It's our job to show you your stunning beauty."

Alice touched her face. Still no reflection. *How extraordinary! Thank goodness the maidservants can see me.*

Lacie guided Alice to lean back against the chair. "Just sit back and let us be your mirror. Let us show you how gorgeous you are by letting us adore you with our attention and admiration."

Alice eased into the seat and settled down, allowing her confusion to drip away. With the hot lights still upon her, she welcomed the cooling sponges stroking her skin. La brought more milk from the basin to rinse Alice's hair. Lacie and Ice sponged her breasts.

Alice breathed out a relaxing sigh.

They sponged her belly.

She sank deeper into the chair.

They sponged her thighs, her shins.

She lost herself to memories of when she was a child sleeping safely in her mother's lap.

They sponged her ankles, her feet.

She let their massage of adoration sink in.

The lights dimmed off and on in a slow, steady pattern.

"What's going on?" Alice asked.

Lacie smirked. "It seems you're arousing the lumen."

Her gaze flitted from statue to statue, the lights from their mouths changing back and forth between dim and bright, as if panting. She gasped. "You mean they're alive?"

"Of course they're alive," Mistress Ice said. "All lumen are alive. Lacie, fetch the corset and gown."

Alice scowled. This changed everything. She no longer felt a sense of privacy. She had an audience. Yet she had no urge to cover herself.

Lacie handed a coral gown to Mistress Ice and held up a white corset in front of Alice. "Ready for you."

Alice stood defiantly, faced the huffing lumen, and puffed her chest out. *Enjoy me while you can.*

Lacie helped Alice into the corset. She felt La tug the strings tight behind her. The corset fit snug against her ribs and pushed up her breasts.

"Now the gown." Mistress Ice gave the gown to La.

La draped the gown over Alice's head. The puffy sleeved gown had a square, low-cut neckline. The top edge of the corset peeked out playfully. The front slit in the skirt would make walking easy, and show off her creamy thighs with every step.

The lights dimmed and brightened at a faster pace, now, panting heavier. She moistened between her legs and her heart pumped. The maidens weren't the only ones that made her feel beautiful and sexy.

Lacie applied a brush to Alice's cheeks. Lacie wore such a proud smile as she scrutinized Alice's face. La brushed Alice's hair with long, gentle sweeps. Alice sighed with pleasure.

"Raise your arms to the side, my lady," Mistress Ice said.

Alice spread her arms out.

La and Ice tugged elbow-length silky gloves onto her hands and up her arms, up past her elbows. The sparkly coral gloves matched her dress. With a tiny brush, Lacie stroked lipstick along Alice's lips. Alice smacked her lips together to make sure the lipstick coated evenly. She gasped at the taste.

"Miss?" La asked.

"I didn't know lipstick could taste like giggles." She licked her lips and giggled. The taste was catching.

Ice placed a pair of coral shoes at Alice's feet. "The last of the outfit."

Alice slipped into the kitten heels and smiled. "What, no underwear?"

Lacie laughed. "My dear, you won't be needing any for the coronation. They'll just get in the way."

Ice stepped back and looked Alice up and down.

Alice asked, "Admiring your handiwork?"

Ice smiled. "No, my dear. I'm admiring you."

Alice's heart warmed. She licked her lips, tasted the lipstick again, and giggled.

Ice took her hand. "Now let's get you to your throne."

The maidens escorted Alice into a noisy, chandelier-lit room the size of her bedroom. Like a bride entering the place of the wedding, Alice only saw the backs of everyone's heads.

She scowled at the tiny space. "This hardly seems the festivity I expected."

The room was crowded with nearly a dozen people sitting in rows of chairs split by a single aisle. But Alice thought there would be more than just a dozen people to honor her crowning achievement. The people didn't even notice her enter since they were all facing away. They chatted loudly at each other, as though each one were trying to outdo the other. It made the noise of their chatter rather unbearable.

Alice slapped her gloved hands over her ears.

The rows of chairs on each side spread out atop an oceanic carpet that seemed to splash and quiver like a body of water, yet the aisle in the center was covered in fine beach sand. The aisle of sand led to the front where three thrones perched on a platform. On the left throne sat Queen Carol. On the right throne sat Alice's sister Lois, also dressed as a queen. Between the two of them, the grandest of the three thrones was empty and waiting for her.

"Are you ready?" a man's voice said loudly.

Alice turned and beamed. "Jackyll!"

"Let's announce your arrival." He held up a bagel shaped like a lower case letter "a," then bit off the top of the letter "a" making it look more like a "u." The bagel seemed to harden into brass and uncoiled until the bagel transformed into bugle. Jackyll put the bugle to his lips and blared out notes that sounded more like laughing hyenas.

The attendees hushed and turned. Upon seeing Alice, they all stood and cheered.

Jackyll raised his palms up to quiet the crowd. Was it just Alice's imagination or were there dozens more people in the room?

"It is time for the coronation," Jackyll announced and turned to Alice. "Is there anything you'd like to say, Your Highness?"

Alice studied all the expectant faces and smiled when she recognized many of them. There was the woman from the train, and all the men who'd sung to her. A reminder for Alice to rely on herself to become the woman she wanted to be. There was the blind man who was no longer blind, the one who had taught her to treat herself sweetly. There was Lucy who seemed pleased wearing peasant clothing, a warning for Alice to remember how beauty had its faults, and standing next to Lucy, as if to challenge all Lucy represented, was Roger who looked as stunning as ever, dressed the way he wished to be treated.

Uniquus and Leo were behaving well, perhaps demonstrating how two could get along if only they focused on their common desires. And magnificent Hyde, the very man who helped her realize that every part of her past, the excellent and the horrible, contributed to make her the woman she was today, the woman Jack loved.

Hyde smiled with a trace of sadness in his eyes. Perhaps Hyde was so happy he had tears. There sure were a lot of people watching her!

"Um," Alice wrung her hands and cleared her throat. "Thanks for coming."

The audience hollered with joy. The left and right sides of the room seem to be extending, more chairs appearing, and more guests standing and applauding in front of their chairs. By the walls stood even more guests, people she didn't recognize. Some looked like coal miners, some looked like peasants, some looked like puppets on strings, some looked like fishermen, some looked like drunkards holding chalices up as if toasting Alice's words.

Alice's cheeks heated with embarrassment. She hadn't really said anything very meaningful, yet thanking them for coming garnished great applause.

Jackyll hushed the audience again. "Let us begin."

The three maidens appeared, each holding a queen's ceremonial items. The crowd, still facing Alice who stood at the back of the room, gasped with awe. Mistress Ice approached Jackyll. She held a red velvet pillow sporting a bejeweled crown of many colors.

Jackyll picked up the crown and held it high. "Alice, for the creativity of your imagination, we treasure you."

Alice bowed and let Jackyll place the gorgeous crown atop her head.

La offered a scepter and orb to Jackyll.

Jackyll kissed Alice's right hand. "Alice, for the bravery to face your challenges, we admire you."

Alice accepted the scepter with her right hand.

Jackyll kissed her left hand. "Alice, for the wit and wisdom you offer, we cherish you."

Alice accepted the orb in her left hand.

Lacie handed Jackyll a red and white velvet cloak.

Jackyll stepped behind Alice. "Alice, for the beauty you hold, both inside and out, we see you."

He embraced her, wrapping her in the cloak. The crowd cried out in cheers and applause.

Jack spoke gently at her ear. "Let me accompany

you to your throne," he squeezed her tighter, "Your Majesty."

Alice filled with warmth at his embrace.

He moved to her side and offered his arm. She smiled and took it.

"Oh, just a second." Alice slipped off her coral shoes. "I want to enjoy this."

They stepped onto the aisle of sand, the warm sand shifting deliciously between her toes. Alice could no longer see the walls to her left and to her right. The distance of the ends of the room seemed to be overcrowded with hundreds upon hundreds of spectators. They were all here for her. Her heart flowed with gladness. She walked down the aisle enjoying the sand under her bare feet, but the more she advanced, the longer the aisle seemed to stretch.

"Jackyll, is it just me, or is the aisle getting longer?"

Jackyll nodded. "Haven't you ever noticed how walking on sand can slow you down?"

Alice scowled. "Yes."

"Well, there you are then."

She gulped. Would she ever get to the throne? Having sand slow you down was one thing but stretching the actual path was quite another. She dismissed her worry and smiled at the crowd. Their cheers and shouts of appreciation invigorated her. The adulation they showered upon her as she strolled with Jackyll was wonderful.

The sand was no longer a hindrance and in no time at all, she found herself in front of the empty throne.

Jackyll bowed and gestured to the throne. "Your Majesty."

Was she supposed to curtsy? Alice wasn't sure. She curtsied anyhow and sat between Queen Lois and Queen Carol. "Thank you, Jackyll."

Jackyll smiled and stepped back. Queen Carol gently gripped Alice's hand. "How was your adventure, Alice?"

"Life-changing," Alice said, smiled, and turned to her sister. "Lois, about what happened in the Forgotten Forest—"

Queen Lois cut in. "We didn't recognize each other." She brushed it away with a wave of her hand. "Milk under the bridge."

Alice sighed with relief.

Jackyll bowed again. "My queen, with your permission, may I be the first to offer you my services?"

Not sure what that meant, Alice said, "It would be an honor."

The audience applauded, pumping their fists in the air and cheering.

Jackyll went down on his knees and gently parted Alice's dress.

Alice gasped.

Oh, geez. Was this what he meant by servicing

her?

Queen Carol snapped her fingers. "Guards! Follow suit!"

Lois and Carol spread their legs for the two knights who went down on their knees and moved in to orally service their queens.

Jackyll looked up at Alice as if waiting. "My queen?"

Alice realized she hadn't opened her legs. "Oh. Of course." She took a deep breath. Being fully appreciated required much more bravery than she had anticipated. These weren't just lumen seeing her naked. These were flesh and blood beings with opinions and judgments soon to see her express her intimate emotions, emotions so personal she only revealed them to Jack in bed.

Alice breathed again and spread her legs.

The spectators cheered and roared.

Jackyll kissed the inside of her thighs, moving closer to Alice's core.

Carol moaned. The guard between her legs must have had talented tasting skills.

Queen Carol said, "I have one more riddle for you, Alice."

Alice felt Jackyll's tongue tease her, circling around her folds. She grinned and sighed at the delicious sensations, her tension easing a bit. "What is the riddle?"

Jackyll's tongue traced Alice's clit. She gasped.

Queen Carol recited:

> *None claim to have it, though everyone does.*
> *At home, it is secretly placed.*
> *Occasionally someone shows his to the world,*
> *And all must respond with distaste.*

Jackyll sucked in her folds. Alice squirmed and hummed with pleasure.

> *After they scoff and they scold the brave man,*
> *At home, they seek out what they shun.*
> *They unlock their dark secret of having a stock,*
> *Some have many, and some just have one.*

Jackyll kissed Alice's pussy, penetrating her with his lustful tongue. Her excitement dripped into his mouth as she tried to pretend she wasn't in front of hundreds of spectators. Lord, he felt so good.

> *It's made by a master who fights with a blade*
> *Stabbing until the host cries.*
> *A translucent blood will drain out from the one*
> *Who owns the dark secret and dies.*

Jackyll pushed his tongue deeper inside Alice. She knew what he was seeking. By the way her heart pounded in furious gulps and her breath heaved, she knew he'd find the proof of her pleasure soon.

Like snow, it will cause the possessor to shudder.
Like faults, it will make her land quake.
And though it can bring about faces of pain,
Everyone longs to partake.

Jackyll waved his fingertips across Alice's clit and delved deeper into her with his tongue. She granted him the treasure he sought, locking his head between her thighs, clutching his head and pushing him as close she could against her pussy. His tongue, so skillful, his fingers, so lithe.

Alice knew the answer to Carol's riddle. It was easy.

She panted. Then her thunder and lightning shook from her upper body, through her pounding heart, and pulsed down her core all into Jackyll's mouth. Just as he desired. Just as she desired.

She cried out in delight and panted the answer. "An orgasm."

"Quite right," Queen Carol replied, sucking in her own climax.

Jackyll dabbed his glistening, grateful grin with a handkerchief and stepped back.

"Stop this," a voice shouted from the back of the room. "The queen will die!"

Alice opened her eyes. It was the black knight, Alice's own shadow, fully armed and scowling. The knight climbed over guests wielding a sword. Some tried to stop her. She cut and sliced and ran them through with her weapon.

"Stop this at once!" The black knight cried and butchered her way through the rows of spectators. "Or Queen Alice will die!"

Alice froze, stiff from fear. Jackyll also didn't move. Lord, what was she going to do?

Hyde rushed to the back of the room and planted himself in the line between the knight and Alice.

"It's too late." Hyde raised his own sword. "She's made her decision."

"You're worse than Jackyll," the black knight said and drove her sword through Hyde's chest to the very hilt.

Hyde collapsed to his knees.

"No!" Alice cried.

Queen Carol snapped her fingers. "Guards, stop that knight."

A flurry of guards rushed to fight the black knight. They brandished their swords and shields. The knight sliced through one guard and pummeled another with the hilt of her sword. She parried their swings, blocking their swords with her own, and flipped in summersaults over their heads.

The remaining guards attempted to get close enough to Alice to shield her, but the black knight was too nimble for them and was much closer to Alice than they were.

Jackyll pounced in front of Alice, facing the black knight with a dagger gripped in one hand. The blade shook.

"D—D—Don't come any closer," Jack said.

The black knight sneered, "Worthless idiot." She lunged and sliced his throat in one swift move.

Jackyll fell to the ground, blood pooling around him.

Alice screamed.

The woman pounced on Alice's throne, threw her sword to the ground with a clatter, and gently placed her hands on Alice's cheeks.

With a piercing gaze, the knight whispered, "You must stop this."

23. Crowned in the Library

If you have helpful advice for someone,
Perhaps the advice you have is for yourself.

J ACK woke up gasping for breath. Where was he? He wiped the sweat off his forehead and noticed the bookshelves around him.

Now he remembered.

After he had finished preparing the fires in the mansion, he'd sought out Alice to break up with her and give her the chance to find a better man. She'd been in the library, asleep on the couch. When he tried to wake her, she just muttered something unintelligible and turned over on her side.

He had decided to be there for her when she woke up, so he lay on the floor beside her.

Jack sat up to check the couch. Alice still lay asleep there. Good.

He yawned. The wall clock let him know that it was quarter past ten in the morning. He'd only been asleep for twenty minutes. Good. He still had plenty of time before he needed to be in the kitchen to help the cook prepare lunch. He checked his palm. The wound from the branch that pierced him when he had prepared the dining room fire was healing well.

What a crazy dream! Considering how uncomfortable the floor was, it came as no surprise that such a wild dream had disturbed his sleep.

Usually he had to work at trying to remember his dreams, but this one stuck with him clearly. As bizarre as the dream was, Jack recognized its value.

Alice slept on her back. Under her yellow dress, her breasts rose and fell with each steady breath. She was sleeping soundly. His cock stirred. He resisted the urge to slide his hands under her neckline and claim handfuls of her cleavage.

Her arm dangled off the couch. The ring he'd won at the fair for her lay on the floor. Perhaps it had slipped off her finger? He picked it up and tucked it in his back pocket, the same pocket that held his leather gloves, her lovely gift to him.

Glancing at those amazing breasts, he steered his lustful hands to her hair instead, and gently stroked her locks away from her face, hoping that would wake her.

"Wake up, Alice," he whispered. "I understand now."

She moaned. Her eyes fluttered into consciousness. With her lids half-closed, she licked her dry lips and swallowed.

"What time is it?" She squinted at the room.

"It's after ten in the morning. Listen, Alice. I understand what you meant by wanting to be treated like a queen." Jack ran his fingers through her blonde locks. "It's not that you wanted to be given jewelry and expensive gifts. You just wanted to be appreciated."

She gazed at him, wide-eyed, fully awake now, giving him her full attention.

"Alice, I know that there's a good chance you'll change and become a different person." Jack studied Alice's face, making sure she understood his words. "But what you enjoy doing, or reading, or eating, those are not the reasons why I love you. I love you because you're so creative. And your creativity is one thing that will never change."

She showed no signs of confusion, no scowls, no shrugs. Instead, her eyes welled. There was much more to say.

He gulped. *How do I say this?* He puffed out a breath and dove in, eyeing her luscious lips.

"I know I haven't been giving you the attention

you deserve. You're right to be upset by that." He shifted his gaze to her supple breasts. Acting on his desires could help allay the grief he caused her. "Can I show you how I truly feel?"

Alice said nothing. Now she scowled as if trying to translate his words. She nodded.

He stood and positioned himself on the couch over Alice, a knee on either side of her hips.

She said nothing, still scowling and watching his face.

He lay on top of her, caressing her hair. He recalled the honey be's in his dream.

"I admire you, Alice. You will always be admired."

He kissed her forehead. She gazed up at him wide-eyed.

"I cherish you, Alice. You will always be cherished."

He kissed her cheeks, first one then the other. He could feel her breath deepening beneath his chest.

"I treasure you. You will always be treasured."

He kissed her neck, tasting a hint of sweat there. She moaned.

"I adore you. So much." He kissed her lips.

She returned the kiss with a passion that made him harden. He adjusted himself.

The kiss deepened. He tasted her delicate lips and urgent tongue. She moved beneath him, her hips shifting up to him. He ground against her, entwining his tongue with hers.

Damn, how he wanted to hike up that bloody dress of hers and pound his cock into her pussy, ram himself into her and make her cry out in pleasure. But he had to stay true to what she wanted. She wanted to be treated like a queen, and though his cock had different ideas at the moment, her happiness mattered most.

He broke the kiss and together they panted, catching their breath. Jack shifted himself down her legs, moving his face closer to her chest. He licked his lips at the billowing of her breasts.

I may not have the joy of impaling her with my cock, but at least I can satisfy my lustful hands.

He reached underneath her neckline and his cock twitched as he squeezed handfuls of those tantalizing breasts.

ALICE moaned, her breasts delighting in Jack's affection. Her mind still sifted through waking up to Jack's strange remarks.

If Jack thought I wanted him to buy me expensive gifts all the time, no wonder he responded by saying he couldn't treat me like a queen.

Jack tugged the neckline down and freed her breasts out of their bra cups, exposing them to the cool air of the library.

Alice took in a deep breath, her chest filling with anticipation.

"I desire you." He placed his hot mouth on a nipple and swirled his wet tongue around, passing along the desire straight into her.

As he stirred her arousal to life, she remembered how vague she had been with her request.

How did Jack realize that when I told him I wanted to be treated like a queen, I meant that I wished he'd give me more of his attention and devotion?

Jack popped his lips off her nipple. "I crave you."

Desire? Crave? Why is he choosing those words?

He switched to her other nipple, and his tongue sparked a drooling hunger that dripped at her core.

Alice moaned.

He pressed his stiff bulge against her thigh, and her questions about his choice of words drifted like smoke, up and away.

Alice watched him taking a mouthful of her flesh between his lips, his thick shoulders covered by that red and black plaid shirt and the straps of his olive-green overalls. She put her hands on his head and undulated against his bulge, desiring him, craving him.

This is what I missed.

He sucked on her nipple. With deft hands, reached under her skirt and tugged down her damp panties. Alice helped by kicking them off her ankles.

He released her moistened nipple into the chill of the air. She shivered at the pleasure of the cool air on her breasts and let the combination of the cool air and her hot desire harden her nipples even more.

Alice put a hand to her heart, reassuring the thumping thing that it would soon have a lot more to thump about by the look of the grin on Jack's face.

He shifted up to her, his face a breath away from hers. She grinned back at him.

His hands caressed her hair once more, and his eyes submerged into her soul. She gasped as she felt him bow to her heart.

"Most of all, Alice, you need to know this." His nostrils flared. "I see you."

Alice's heart cracked open and let him in. *This is what I missed.*

He kissed her with delicate lips.

This.

Alice met his kiss and demanded more. She wrapped her arms around his head, feeling that thick thatch of black hair twine around her fingers.

And this.

He pulled back from the kiss. "Let me show you."

He shifted his body again, lining up his head with her waist. Alice raised her eyes to the ceiling as she realized what he set out to do next. Jack parted her thighs and placed loving kisses between them. Alice's heart hammered faster. She put her hands over her heart.

See? I told you he'd give us a lot more to thump about.

He licked her clit, swirled his tongue around it, giving Alice the attention she craved.

Alice gasped. She cupped her breasts, warming away the chill of her moistened nipples, and kneaded them with delight.

Jack licked her folds, taking them into his mouth and flicking them between his lips.

Alice swallowed, feeling herself drip onto Jack's chin and between her legs.

I must be spilling all over the couch. She squeezed her breasts and squirmed under Jack's skillful tongue, letting the sparks fly. *Good.*

He plunged his tongue inside her, swirling around, stirring her juices.

Alice quivered.

He pushed his tongue deeper.

Alice shook.

He grabbed her thighs.

Alice pinched her nipples with a cry and pressed her pussy into his face.

He pushed his flat tongue against her clit with strong licks.

Alice stiffened. Her orgasm hit through her with a delicious wave. She screamed and undulated, writhing and squirming on his tongue. That kept going, bringing her higher.

She slammed her hands to her sides and clenched the couch. She kicked out and curled her toes. Another wave washed through her. She had no choice but to let the amazing sensation take its course.

The rolling orgasm rippled away. Her pussy pulsed. Alice sank into the couch and heaved heavy breaths.

Jack lifted his head, grinning. "You okay?"

Alice giggled and nodded, too breathless to reply.

She had to find out how Jack came to realize she missed his attention and needed to hear why he loved her. And desire? Crave? Why did he choose those words?

JACK climbed on top of Alice on the couch and kissed her gently. She kissed him back, then licked his lips, smiling up at him.

Knowing that she tasted her own tart self on his lips aroused him further. He growled. His cock was eager to explode, but for now, this was about her. Loving her, adoring her, giving her all she desired and not forgetting to show his gratitude anymore.

He lay beside her, her neckline still down and her breasts still spilling out of her bra. She cuddled against him and he tucked an arm around her, holding her close.

"Jack?" She traced a finger on his shirt.

"Mm?"

"I had a dream last night about honey bees. They said the same thing you did just now when you made love to me."

What in the bloody hell?

"Are you serious?" Jack propped himself on his elbow and checked her expression to make sure she wasn't pulling an elaborate trick of some sort. No smirk, no sneaky sparkle in her eye. She was serious. "You had the same dream I did?"

"Uh…" She narrowed her eyes. "You also dreamed that you were surrounded by honey bees?"

"Not me," Jack shook his head. "You. The whole dream was about you. That is, I *was* in the dream. I showed up a lot, even as twins called Jackyll and Hyde. But the dream was really about you. Getting out of the library, meeting Queen Carol, taking a journey from square to square to get to your coronation."

Alice gasped. "Lord! We really had the same dream?" She covered her face with her hands but her blush still showed prettily. "So you saw me do—" She bit her lip. "Everything?"

Jack chuckled. "Yes, I saw you with Lois in the Forgotten Forest, and all your sexual adventures with Jackyll, Hyde, Uniquus, and the others." He kissed her. "You can bet I'll enjoy reflecting on those fond memories for years to come."

"Oh, for goodness sake!" Alice laughed and covered her face with her hands. She then gasped and pulled her hands away, her face beaming. "So that's how you knew what I meant when I said I wanted to be treated like a queen."

He lay his head back down and stared up at the ceiling. "Exactly. Throughout your entire adventure you sought to be adored. When I woke up, I thought the dream was my subconscious figuring out what you meant, but I guess the dream was really your own subconscious."

"True. I did learn a lot." Alice wore a wicked grin. "But I didn't get the answers to everything."

"What do you mean?"

Alice asked sweetly, "Remember when Hyde said you had a hidden side?"

Oh, bloody hell.

Alice trailed a finger across his shirt, up and down his chest, and continued using her sing-song voice. "What was that about?"

Jack thought of the gloves in his back pocket. "Uh, you don't want to know."

This time it was Alice's turn to prop herself up on her elbow. "Oh, yes," Alice grinned and nodded. "Yes, I most certainly do."

Those leather gloves on Alice's creamy white skin. Jack's chin itched hot. "No, you don't."

"Did you steal a famous painting of a dog playing solitaire with five other lonely dogs?"

"No," Jack chuckled.

"Did you kill a wicked German who turned out to be a mannequin modeling the latest fashion in lederhosen?"

"No." Jack didn't want to tell her his secret, but this had to be the most entertaining third degree ever.

Alice's eyes widened. "Do you secretly work for Her Majesty's Secret Service jumping out of airplanes over Switzerland to fetch the queen fresh Swiss cheese? Were you a pirate with a hook for a hand that ate so many salamanders that your hand grew back? Oh, I know! You're a possum disguised as a human and you're afraid to admit your love of girly Monet paintings."

Jack shook his head while laughing.

"Well, if you're not any of those, what could possibly be left?"

There was no stopping her. If Alice had her heart set out to find an answer, she wouldn't stop until she found it. Jack had to tell her. Or perhaps… "Alright. You really want to know?"

Alice beamed. "Yes, Jack. I really want to know."

"Very well." Jack stood and strolled across the room. "Perhaps the best way is to show you."

"Intriguing!" Alice rubbed her hands together.

He locked the library door with his set of house keys, turned to her, and said cheerfully, "How about we play a game of Simon Says?"

The only others with the key to the library were Alice's father and Barbara the maid. Jack knew their routines well enough to know neither would disturb them.

Alice eyed the locked door and scowled. "Simon Says? Now?"

"Do you want to see my hidden side or not?" Jack strode back to her and urged her to her feet.

"I do, I do!"

He loved the way she tucked her breasts back into her bra and dress.

"Then trust me." Facing her, he took both her hands in his own and led her to the center of the library.

Alice smirked.

He let go of her hands and stepped back. "Ready?"

She put her hands on her waist. "Sure."

Jack remembered the dream. Alice had fantasies of playing a naughty game of Simon Says when she came upon Roger, the man who sat on a wall. The game would be a good way of them both getting what they wanted. He only hoped Alice wouldn't be too shocked or disgusted by his hidden side.

*****

ALICE waited for her instructions. What was Jack up to?

"Simon says take one step forward."

Alice rolled her eyes and complied.

Jack nodded and smiled, looking pleased with himself. "Simon says take two steps forward."

Alice smirked at the ridiculous game and stepped twice closer to Jack, arriving at an arm's length from him.

"Simon says take two more steps forward."

But then she'd be practically up against him. Alice snickered. Oh, so that was his plan. To tease him, she took two tiny steps forward.

He smirked. "Closer."

Alice stood her ground.

Jack pursed his lips and nodded as though impressed. "I didn't say 'Simon says.' Good job." He crossed his arms across his chest. "Now, let's get down to business. Simon says take off your shoes and stand on my feet."

Stand on his feet? That didn't sound sexy. She used her toes to slip off her yellow flats, stepped up to him, and climbed onto his work boots. She had to grab hold of his crossed arms to balance herself.

Though she was stable now, she felt herself leaning backwards. If she let go of Jack's arms, she'd fall.

Jack didn't move. Alice stayed there, peering up at

his gorgeous face. He no longer looked stern as he did in the beginning of the game. He now looked loving, his blue eyes gazing at her with adoration.

"Alice," he whispered, "Simon says get on your knees."

Alice sucked in a breath. Her heart pumped faster. Was he giving her a choice?

"Simon says," Jack over-enunciated, "get – on – your – knees."

Alice gulped. She stepped off his feet and clung to Jacks overalls for balance as she descended to the ground.

"Simon says," Jack unfastened his overalls and let them fall to his ankles, exposing his white boxers with a blue diamond pattern, "take out my cock."

Alice clenched her thighs detecting her moistness, and peered up at him. His hands were on his waist. His face remained gentle even though he spoke with such a commanding tone. She bit her lip and reached into his boxers. She gripped his stiff cock. Its heat warmed her palm. She flipped it out from under his waistband and licked her lips.

He slipped the boxers off his waist and they fell on top of his overalls at his ankles.

Lord, she loved looking at his cock. She wanted to trace the crown with her fingertips. The crown of King Jack.

And here she was, not treated like a queen but like an obedient subject.

He unbuttoned the top buttons of his wool shirt, then tugged it over his head and cast it to the floor.

"Simon says," he paused.

That lingering moment stirred a liquid ache inside her.

Simon says what? Touch it? Lick it? Fuck my ear with it? Tell me and I'll do anything you say.

He said, "Suck my cock."

She took him in her mouth and gulped down as much of him as she could.

He groaned.

Hearing his pleasure delighted her and triggered a spike of need of her own. She cupped herself and rubbed at that itch.

This was so unlike Jack. The closest he ever came to asking her for a blowjob before was by saying, *Alice, could you pleasure me with that amazing mouth of yours?* He'd always been so polite. But not today. And that turned her on.

She swirled her tongue around his cock, sucking, feasting on him like she'd been a starving servant and he was gracious enough to offer her sustenance.

Alice had no idea what has happening to her. Jack was supposed to be the servant to her family, not the other way around. And she wasn't supposed to enjoy being treated like a servant. Such things were improper.

She didn't care.

She lapped hungrily on King Jack's staff and stopped rubbing herself. Her breasts needed her attention. She pinched her nipples through her dress as though they were tickled pink at how inappropriate she'd become and needed a good pinching.

He placed his hands on her head. "Simon says fuck me with your mouth." His gruff words sounded as hungry as she was.

She bobbed her head on his cock, his hands guiding her rhythm. She kept a hand on her breast and reached back between her thighs for her clit. Rubbing herself there let the lust in her heart find its way to her core. But so did the guilt.

This was wrong, wasn't it?

She ignored the thought and rubbed herself faster.

Jack applied more pressure on her head and thrust into her throat. *Lord, he's going deep without checking in on me. It's like he's losing control.*

Mm, yes.

She smiled against his cock and sucked harder.

His desire for her made him lose control. Knowing she had that power over him spilled out from between her thighs and onto her fingers.

He thrust deeper. He held her head against his waist, mashing her face against his musky patch of curly hair, as if to say, *Mine. You are all mine.* His thick staff of flesh tapped the back of her throat. A choking sensation built up. His hands confined her head there, her throat stuffed and gagging.

She pulled herself off his cock and turned aside. "Stop!"

He staggered back, his hands up in surrender. He looked aghast like he'd done a horrible thing.

It was incredible. As much as he had lost control of himself with his desire for her, she had still been able to stop him and had power over him.

Did she really want to be treated this way? Her body dripped and tingled and pleaded with her to continue.

Alice let out a nervous smile. "I didn't say, 'Simon says stop.' "

Jack shifted his head and peered at her as if making sure she was being truthful.

She opened her mouth and closed her eyes.

JACK couldn't believe it. He took in the sight of Alice, his employer's daughter, on her knees with her eyes closed and her mouth open, waiting to take his cock between her lips.

His employer's daughter. Jack's adrenalin kicked in at the power he felt.

His cock had gone limp when Alice told him to

stop. He thought he might have hurt her. That was the last thing he wanted.

Now, seeing her on her knees, stirred the arousal and quickened his pulse. He stroked his cock, returning it to full attention.

The reason for his lust was wrong. He knew that. He shouldn't feel so aroused at having such control over a woman just because she was the daughter of his boss. But what surprised him was that Alice played along with his fantasy. True, he hadn't told her what his arousal stemmed from, how having his cock in his boss's daughter's throat got his blood pumping hard, but the way she was on her knees, mouth open, eyes closed, it proved she had a willingness to love him, quirks and all. And that made his adoration for Alice grow fonder.

He peeled off his boots, hopping on one free foot, then the other, and yanked his overalls and boxers off his ankles. Alice remained in her pose, but it looked like she was breathing more heavily. Anticipating him, perhaps? She peeked through one eye and smiled at his clumsy strip dance.

He stepped up to her and guided himself into her mouth.

She kept her eyes closed, placed her hands around his thighs, and pulled him in closer. Jack felt reassured by her gesture. She wanted this.

Her tongue danced along the underside of his cock and swirled around his tip.

He grabbed her head, carefully fisted thick locks of her hair, and pushed himself into her throat. He gripped her hair as if holding onto horns and thrust faster. Her mouth felt incredible, igniting all sorts of fires in his cock.

The back of her throat twitched around him, squeezing his tip deliciously. Her tongue pressed against his underside.

I'm in her mouth. My cock is stuffed inside Alice's mouth.

That source of her spoken wit and imagination now pushed his cock into a higher state of need.

He slipped in and out faster. His muscles tightened. He plunged down her throat and held her head against his waist, bursting. He ground his teeth and sucked in his breath to keep from screaming.

Alice grabbed his waist and pushed him deeper into her mouth. Her every swallow massaged his spurting cock. It was too much pleasure. He cried out, releasing himself vocally as much as he released into her throat.

The final dribbles escaped his tip. Alice's hot tongue swirled around, catching the last drops.

Jack eased back, flopping out from her lips. Even after all she'd swallowed, a drop ran down her chin. She peered up at him breathing heavily and wiped off the escaping drop with the back of her hand.

Jack fell to his knees and clutched her arms. He stared at her eyes.

Does she realize how much I adore her?

He gazed deeper, as though exploring every inch of her soul through her eyes could help him sink into her further and understand her in ways he never could before.

I need to show her. Always.

He embraced her, holding her as close to himself as possible.

He ran his hands across her back, holding every part of her against him. Closer. Closer, still.

Alice clung to him as if he were her last hope and would never let him go. He could feel her heart fluttering. She shuddered in his arms.

Was she excited? Nervous? Scared? Whatever she felt, she had the power to stop him at any time.

He whispered at her ear, "I'm not done with you, yet."

Jack stood and offered Alice his hand. She accepted it. He helped her up off the floor.

She rubbed her knees.

Jack took her by the nape of her neck and kissed her hard. She seemed to go limp, so he caught her lower back and pressed her against him to keep her from falling.

He loved the feel of her delicate lips.

He let her go and she staggered back. "Simon says stand facing the wall with your shoulders up against it."

He removed the pair of leather gloves from his

back pocket. Time to see if his fantasy was as titillating in reality as he'd dreamed.

ALICE'S mind filled with salacious questions as she saw Jack take out the gloves she had given him as a gift. What was he going to do with those?

"Well?" Jack gestured to the wall.

Alice's face flushed hot. She turned to face the wall, and leaned into it. She turned her head to see through the corner of her eye what he was up to.

"Simon says," he wiggled his fingers into each glove, "reach behind you and hitch the back of your skirt over your waist."

Alice's heart hammered at his command. Was her body warning her against obeying him? Or was she so overcome with desire that she mistook it for fear? All she knew was she had no interest in analyzing her feelings. The moistness between her thighs called for satisfying more urgent needs.

With her cheek against the cold wall, she arched her back and raised her yellow skirt over her hips, baring her bottom in the chilly library air.

Jack stepped up behind her and stood to one side of her. He glided his leather fingertips across her flesh, then rubbed his flat leather-covered palm along the curves of her backside. She shivered in delight. The leather felt more exciting than she had anticipated.

Alice glanced over her shoulder at Jack, and loved the way he couldn't tear his eyes from her rear. A look of lust oozed out of him. He squeezed her flesh, spreading her apart, opening her up. Her heart pounded harder, forging excitement with its clamoring beats.

That look of lust told her more than just how he felt. It also told her that the way he touched her came from a place of his raw desire, his primal urge to please himself, not just a desire to make her happy.

He cupped her mound and pressed his leather palm against her clit.

Mmm. He touches me there because he wants to. His look of lust confesses it.

He flicked his fingers across her folds.

She bit her lip. *He wants to touch me like this. His lust confesses it.*

He pushed a leather finger inside her.

Alice moaned.

He stirred her around, that slick leather sliding inside.

Alice bunched her skirt behind her in her fists. So incredible.

He wants this, too. Who I am makes him want this.

He plunged a second finger in and growled.

Lord, he actually growled from it! His fingers

inside filled her. She clenched around his fingers, dripping down her thighs, letting him do what he wanted.

He pulled out and stood behind her. Reaching around her torso, he grabbed the neckline of her dress and ripped it open, the sound of threads tearing filled the library.

Alice gasped. She was getting a glimpse at just how much he wanted her.

He yanked her bra down her shoulders to her belly, her bare breasts jiggled free.

Jack leaned over her and squeezed her breasts from behind. The palms of his leather gloves rubbed circles across her nipples.

Alice's breasts heated. She closed her eyes, letting her excitement and fear rumble through her.

Jack held an arm across her breasts and used his free hand to pummel her pussy with two fingers.

Alice squealed with pleasure at the increased speed.

"You like that, Alice?" Jack plunged into her with rapid thrusts. "Do you?"

"Yes," she admitted. Her body jerked forward with his every plunge.

"Damn, you are so bloody sexy."

Alice writhed. Her muscles stiffened. Her nipples perked. She clenched around his fingers and shouted out her orgasm. Shocks popped inside her. She shook on Jack's fingers, a series of little deaths firing at her pussy, burning her core, searing across her clenched belly, her arched back and shoulders, her balled up fists. It incinerated her into ashes. She trembled.

Her shakes settled.

Her trembling settled.

She quivered.

Her quivering settled and her muscles could no longer hold her.

Jack caught her and eased her to the floor. "I've got you, Alice."

She let herself spill out of Jack's arms and sat on her hip, propped up by one arm. The floor was hard and uncomfortable. What the hell was happening to her?

Jack brushed a curl of hair out of her eyes. "What's wrong?"

Alice scowled. "What we just did. It's wrong, isn't it? My parents raised me to be independent. A woman isn't supposed to be told what to do."

Jack's face hardened. "You mean, like a servant?"

Alice's heart sank into the ashes in her chest. "Oh, no, Jack. I didn't mean it that way. I just—"

"I know what you meant," Jack said holding up his hand to stop her from explaining. "All your life you've been taught to empower yourself by making your own decisions, but here you followed my commands."

Alice nodded and gulped. "More than that. I thought I wanted to be treated like a queen, but instead you treated me in a brutish way."

Jack paled. "I'm sorry, Alice. I should never have shown you that side of me."

"No, Jack." She caressed his rough cheek. "I'm glad you shared that with me. But," knots in her gut tied and twisted, "that's the problem." Bare-chested, she eyed her yellow dress, torn down to her waist, and her bra around her belly, the straps hanging at her elbows.

Jack took her hand and squeezed. "I'm not sure I understand what you mean."

Her torn clothes seemed a fitting packaging for the quality of woman she was. "Jack, I was glad you did that to me."

He eyed her. "You mean, you enjoyed it."

She nodded.

Jack let out a breath. Was he smiling?

Anger surged inside and Alice pushed him away. "I'm serious!"

"I know you are." He regained his balance, but still wore that stupid grin. "I'm just relieved you're not upset with me, that's all."

Alice's lips trembled and her eyes blurred wet. She felt a fluttering among the ashes her orgasm had left inside her. Lord, what had she become?

"Come here," Jack took her into his arms. "I got you," he whispered.

Alice clung onto him on the library floor.

What had she become? How could she enjoy

being treated so rough?

Then she remembered the black knight. At the coronation, it seemed like the woman in black armor wanted to kill her but at the last moment, the knight dropped her sword at Alice's feet. The woman practically pleaded with her to stop. Stop what? Her pursuit of wanting to be a queen?

No.

The knight wanted Alice to stop her pursuit of *being treated* like a queen. The woman knew that's not what Alice wanted.

Alice got goosebumps across her arms as she chipped away at the truth of her dream.

All throughout the dream, Alice delighted in being treated rough, manhandled. The ring on her pinky buzzed every time she had those crude experiences. By seeking out the dominant position of a queen, Alice had been ignoring her true desires.

Alice clung to Jack harder as she chewed on the enigma.

The riddle had said: *The sad truth of it all is, to follow your lie, you must let the secret of your little deaths die.*

Alice followed a belief that she could be happy if she were treated like a queen. While true for many others, that belief for her was a lie. By ignoring her longing to be ravished, Alice was indeed letting her little deaths, her orgasms, die. And when Queen

Carol told her the black knight could wake Alice up, the queen didn't mean the black knight could wake her from her sleep. The queen meant that the black knight could wake her up to her true desires.

Sitting on the floor, Alice felt her breasts press against Jack's chest. The fire of her climax had burned away all the lies and left her with the ashes of her actual longings, her perverse needs. Her pussy shamelessly throbbed at the memory. Though the black knight had failed to arouse her sleeping desires, Jack did a good job of it.

Jack gently nudged her off his chest and peered at her. "What are you thinking?"

"It's wrong, Jack, isn't it?"

"Did it feel wrong?"

Alice let the truth whisper out of her. "No."

Jack took a deep breath and let it out. "I can't say I understand it. But I know that if it feels right for both of us, it can't be wrong." With gentle fingers, he adjusted her bra back over her breasts. "In the meantime, let's be open to it and explore if having this together is what we want. Consider it as an adventure."

Alice smiled a little and wiped at her sniffles. "That sounds like it could be a fun adventure."

Jack chuckled. "Here." He reached into his back pocket and brought out the ring he had won for her at the fair. He took her hand and placed the ring in her open palm. "If you ever want me to play rough with you again, just put on this ring. That way, you won't need to feel any embarrassment asking for it. Okay?"

Alice sighed with relief. She nodded, clenched the ring in her fist, and held it to her heart, the fluttering of a phoenix rising from the ashes within.

Jack kissed her tenderly. Alice's heart warmed. She was awake and ready for her next adventure.

The Poem Closes

Upon a foreign grassy hill
Up in a castle tower,
There lived a queen with lovers three
Who loved her every hour.
They touched and licked and whispered words
To wet her budding flower.

The savage Troy she did adore
His scars were long in size.
Her lover Hyde with supple strength
Spoke words so kind and wise.
His brother Jackyll had a smile
With soft and gentle eyes.

And yet such sessions with her men
She felt they could not stay.
"Oh, do they truly feel a love
And mean each word they say?
Or do they think each touch and kiss
Are orders to obey?"

The queen, she wore her servant's dress.
Her fears she had to quell.
"Take me to the dungeon and
Then chain me in a cell."
"As you wish," the servant said.
"And Queen, I wish you well."

Each lover came to visit her,
A slave inside a cage.
Jackyll glanced and Jackyll left,
No interest did he stage.
When Troy he came to visit her,
His face, it filled with rage.

"You look so much like our queen,
The one that I despise.
So now's my chance to take revenge
For living all these lies.
I'll picture you as if you're Queen
And fill you down to size."

He stuffed his fingers 'twixt her legs
And drilled her hard and wet.
He spun her round and hammered her
To see how deep he'd get.
She moaned at all his penetration
And the pace he set.

"You ordered me to love you. If I
Had a choice, I wouldn't."
He thrust himself far into her
In ways she loved but shouldn't.
He left her chained a-dripping wet
And wanting him but couldn't.

As the tears poured down her cheeks,
Dear Hyde came down to visit.
"Hush, fair maiden. Don't you cry.
I'll hold you if you wish it.
My! You look so much like Queen.
Show me your pain, I'll kiss it."

"My heart," Queen said. "It's cracked in two.
I feel so much alone."
"Mine too," Hyde said. "Our queen is gone.
My heart, it feels like stone.
Let me heal your heart and maybe
That shall heal my own."

He loosened open up her dress
And kissed her aching heart.
His kisses lingered to her breasts
His tongue did twirl and dart.
His fingers lifted up her skirt
And dipped into her part.

Her love for him, it dripped and shook
With every touch he gave.
She found the man she loved the most,
The one she could now save.
And so which would *you* rather be,
A beauty queen or slave?

Author's Note

Hi beautiful reader!

I hope you enjoyed my personal take on *Alice Through the Looking Glass.* I love spending time with Alice and plan on continuing her salacious adventures in several more heart-pounding novels. The next one will be based on the fairy tale "Princess and the Pea," entitled *Alice's Story of O.* It picks up right where we left off in this story. Speaking of *Alice's Erotic Adventures Through the Mirror,* when Alice took a close and hard look at her true desires, that moment of confusion was very near and dear to my heart. Some of my hottest fantasies drift to places that shock even myself. I think we all have an idea of what's proper in the bedroom, but when what we desire is different from what's "proper," a deep inner turmoil can surface. What about you? Do you have desires you try not to dwell on because they may seem too improper?

About the Author

Liz Adams, bestselling author of the erotic fairy tale *Alice's Sexual Discovery in a Wonderful Land*, lives in the San Francisco Bay Area, CA. Her short story *Amy "Red" Riding's Hood*, an erotic version of *Red Riding Hood*, is an Amazon bestseller and winner of Goodreads' Book of the Month for October 2012. Her modern day erotic version of Goldilocks, *Goldie's Locks and the Three Men*, is also a bestseller. Liz studied music and creative writing at UCLA and worked as a freelance model before making her writing her career. In her spare time she cuddles with her husband on the couch to watch her favorite shows and often they work together doing hands-on research for her books.

If you enjoyed *Alice's Sexual Discovery*, please write a review on Amazon and/or Goodreads! Also, Liz would love to know how you heard about her book, so drop her a line at LizAdamsBooks@gmail.com or at her website www.LizAdamsAuthor.com.

Also by

Liz Adams

Fairy Tale Erotica

ALICE'S SEXUAL DISCOVERY IN A WONDERFUL LAND

(Alice's Erotic Adventures Book 1)

What will you discover down the rabbit hole?

ALICE'S STORY OF O:

AN EROTIC RETELLING OF THE PRINCESS AND THE PEA

A Choose-Your-Own-Spice Adventure

(Alice's Erotic Adventures Book 3)

The Happily Ever After is guaranteed,

How you get there is up to you.

ARIEL'S SUPER POWER OF LOVE

Ever wonder what Wonder Woman's love life was like?

GOLDIE'S LOCKS AND THE THREE MEN

(A Modern Erotic Fairy Tale Fantasy for Women)

What if the only way to find the right man

was to instead find the right men?

Short Stories

AMY "RED" RIDING'S HOOD

(Fairy Tale Erotica)

Would you submit to the beast within him?

HANSEL & GRETEL AND THE SEXUAL HUNTER

(A Modern Erotic Fairy Tale)

What if the only one who could save your marriage was

your worst enemy?

ALINA SAID, CALL ME MAYBE

(A Short Romance)

How far would you go letting a stranger caress you in public?

Short Stories in Anthologies
"Squirting Secrets" in *Campus Sexploits 3:
Naughty Tales of Wild Girls in College*
(Out of Print!)

"College Sex with a Foreign Exchange Student, the
Universal Language" in *Campus Sexploits 4*
(Out of Print!)

"The Artist" in Sensexual: A Unique Anthology
2013 Vol 1
(Urban Fantasy)